CHRISTOPH
novels – *Snake*
of the West, T
and *A Divisio.*
collection, *About the Body*. He lives in Cumbria.

CHRISTOPHER BURNS

MRS PULASKA

AND OTHER STORIES

SALT
MODERN
STORIES

CROMER

PUBLISHED BY SALT PUBLISHING 2024

2 4 6 8 10 9 7 5 3 1

First published in Great Britain in 2024 by
Salt Publishing Ltd
12 Norwich Road, Cromer, Norfolk NR27 0AX United Kingdom

www.saltpublishing.com

Salt Publishing Limited Reg. No. 5293401

A CIP catalogue record for this book is available from the British Library

ISBN 978 1 78463 315 8 (Paperback edition)
ISBN 978 1 78463 316 5 (Electronic edition)

Typeset in Granjon by Salt Publishing

Printed and bound in Great Britain by Clays Ltd, St Ives plc

For Paul, and in memory of Judy, June, and Iain

Contents

Mrs Pulaska

No ONE KNEW where she came from, or why she chose refuge among us. Perhaps she yearned for the tiny villages and small farms of her childhood, now denied to her forever by the forces of history; perhaps she merely sought escape.

For people such as us she was an emissary from an unknown world, a bizarre and wholly self-absorbed stranger with an impenetrable accent. The very planes and set of her face were different to the ones we were used to. She was angular, with bony features and long black hair like a witch's. For my school friends and me she was a figure of both fear and scorn. We imagined she might be German, and for us all Germans were still enemies.

But her name was Mrs Pulaska, and she was Polish. Of Mr Pulaski, or of a wedding ring, there was no sign. For the time she was with us she lived in a narrow back room at the back of the butcher's shop in the village. Because she always looked cold and undernourished the shopkeepers gave her scraps of food, despite rationing. She wore long-sleeved black clothes even in summer, always with gloves.

In winter she wore woollen mittens, boots, and an outsize greatcoat scavenged from an unidentified army.

When she began to visit our farm I felt both threatened and guilty. I decided that there had been no cause for me to think or say such terrible things about Mrs Pulaska, for I feared that in some obscure way she had come to take revenge.

Instead she ignored me. She spent most of the time in the disused stone barn my father rented to her for a few shillings a week. When better times came, he often said, he would buy one of those new prefabricated buildings, one that would cost little, could be built quickly, and be a lot easier to maintain.

Although Mrs Pulaska had told my father that she wanted to work in the barn I couldn't imagine what kind of work she could do in the cavernous and gloomy interior. But as soon as an agreement was reached she seemed to feel that the building was hers, and she painted the outer door a vivid, fiery crimson.

So every morning Mrs Pulaska would walk down the muddy track to our farm, unlock the crimson door and close it behind her. Often, too, I would see her scouring the fields, mysteriously examining stones or splashing calf-deep in water while she prodded the stream bed with a long stick. Usually she brought back a prize from these foraging missions, and returned cradling a piece of quartz or a length of barbed wire as though they were precious objects. From within the barn came a series of noises that only helped deepen the mystery – the rough scrape of heavy objects dragged across the floor, the muffled bangs of ladders or planking, and a sharply insistent noise, like a thrush's warning call, as if she were a goldsmith beating metal with a tiny hammer.

At our evening meal I asked my father what Mrs Pulaska was building. He told me that she was not a builder but an artist. He spoke the word *artist* as if it were both a puzzle and an affront, and licked his fingers free of chicken fat.

'An artist?' I asked. For me, an artist was someone who drew the pictures in the *Dandy* or the *Beano*.

'If that's what she wants to call herself,' my mother said. 'Just let her.'

'She's no more of an artist than I am,' my father told me. 'She's just a crazy Polish woman, that's all.'

Finished with his part of the bird, he threw the bones into the fire.

'But she's harmless,' my mother said.' Just let her do what she wants to do. Why worry about what she calls herself?'

My father grunted. He could tolerate only a little disagreement, and if ever my mother persisted he would fly into a rage. I had often seen her abandon an argument because she hated his anger; usually I wished that she would stand up to him. The chicken bones, rich with fat, blazed and cracked.

Mrs Pulaska ignored me for months. In bright sunshine or ceaseless rain she always had the same intent, tight, preoccupied expression, as if the only things that mattered were held captive within her own imagination.

One day, however, she caught me spying on her.

My parents had agreed that we would leave her alone and not enter the barn. This made no difference to my

father. He had no use for the building and no interest in whatever Mrs Pulaska was doing. He only knew
that it must be both temporary and irrelevant. But I was
consumed with curiosity.

I had looked at some books in the small public library
– books by artists. Inside I found rich, luxurious images;
lingering studies of disported flesh, sumptuous textures
of skin, breasts, shadow, and hair. Quite suddenly I associated Mrs Pulaska with a kind of sensual comfort and
with nudity. It did not matter that I found her unattractive,
bony, spare; without warning she had become unnervingly
physical. I realised that her body must possess its own secret
history about which I knew nothing.

There was a narrow gap in the door where the planking
had shrunk. Furtive and eager, I pressed my eye against it.

I don't know what I expected to see, but in the event I
saw nothing. A hessian sack had been nailed over the inside
of the door, blocking even a partial view.

As I stood back, crestfallen, Mrs Pulaska bore down
on me across the farmyard, her black hair trailing behind
her like a sign of wickedness. Chickens scattered across the
muddy cobblestones.

I froze with guilt. She put one gloved hand on my
shoulder – not hard, but my imagination turned it into
a fierce grip. I flinched because I thought she was about
to hit me, but instead she merely stared, as though I were
someone that she had never noticed before. Then she let
go and her mouth opened in a sad lopsided smile. There
was blood on her teeth,

She said something I did not understand. Her breath
smelled of dandelions and earth.

'What?' I asked, my voice shaking.

She pointed to the barn and spoke again, but her speech was hobbled and I could only pick out what I thought was the word *wreck*. I nodded rapidly as if I understood, took a few steps to one side, and then turned on my heel and ran away.

Now Mrs Pulaska began returning with other kinds of booty – shards of tile or the ribs and horns from a dead sheep. She began to pester my mother for unwanted cutlery, a smashed plate, or broken glass. Or she would come up the lane pushing a borrowed wheelbarrow containing a bag of cement and a tin of house paint. When my father's friends arrived to slaughter our pig she watched in dismay and then scurried away rather than hear the animal killed. When it began to squeal in terror she was a long way away, a scarecrow in a distant field, but I could see that she covered her ears. Afterwards, however, she asked to be given the bones and the skull.

Winter came early that year. Sleet drove from the skies for days on end and the lanes lay beneath water. Inside the farmhouse the fire burned constantly, even though my father grumbled that the chimney should have been swept long before the weather had turned.

My mother took pity on Mrs Pulaska. One morning she wanted to invite her to eat with us, but my father objected.

The villagers had put an end to their charity, he told her; Mrs Pulaska might be poor, but she could afford to feed herself. Instead of that she squandered her money on ridiculous things, builders' things. If she no longer had free food then perhaps she would see sense.

'But she's ill,' my mother objected. 'Anyone can see that. All you have to do is look at her.'

'So let her feed herself and then go to a doctor,' my father answered.

'Don't be heartless,' my mother pleaded. 'The poor woman probably doesn't know what to do. Would *you* know what to do if you fell ill in Poland and were on your own?'

But my father was stubborn and bitter. 'It's not our fault that she's here. We're not to blame for what's gone on in Europe. It's time she moved on. And that's what she has to do. I told her she could only have the barn temporarily.'

My mother asked what he meant.

There was an envelope on the table where my father did his paperwork. He tipped out the contents – several brochures with plans of prefabricated buildings.

'That's what we want,' he told her. 'We've got to move with the times.'

'But Mrs Pulaska won't understand this,' my mother protested, 'She probably didn't even know what *temporarily* meant. And she's still working in there.'

Furious at having his judgement questioned, my father strode to the front door and opened it.

'I don't care if she's working. I don't care what she's doing. Because whatever it is, she'll have to stop. And I'll make sure she knows exactly what *temporarily* means.'

I sat looking at the fire because I did not want to see my mother's face as she paced the floor.

After a few minutes she went to the door. I followed, still not daring to look at her expression.

Pools of water had collected in the farmyard. My father, his face rigid with shock, was backing away from Mrs Pulaska, who was on her knees in front of him. Her black dress was spattered with mud and animal dirt and her hands were held high in supplication. It was the first time I had seen her bare hands. They were covered in white paint.

As we watched, my father took several more steps backwards. Mrs Pulaska pitched forward and sprawled across the wet cobblestones like someone no longer able to walk. Suddenly she began to cough harshly and repetitively. From her lips came a trickle of blood, bright as the paint on the barn door.

My mother ran across to the sprawled body. 'She needs an ambulance.' She told my father grimly; 'she heeds one now.'

He walked to our telephone as though under protest.

We carried Mrs Pulaska into the house and sat her in a chair in the warmest part of the room. I put another log on the fire while my mother wrapped her in a blanket. Mrs Pulaska had quietened now. She gazed ahead unseeingly, but her face twitched when the log bark cracked as the flames took it. My mother wiped the blood from her chin but as soon as she had done so a little more trickled out of her mouth.

Mrs Pulaska's hands stuck out from under the blanket. The sleeve of her dress had been pushed back and I saw that something had been tattooed on the inside of her wrist. It was a series of numbers that made no sense to me but that stood out in vivid purple against the bloodless skin.

My mother reached forward and pulled the blanket across as if she were covering something shameful. As she did we began to hear a muffled roaring noise. The soot in the chimney had caught fire.

My father looked outside. The wind had dropped and smoke covered the farmyard in a greasy swirling cloud,

We hardly spoke until the ambulance arrived. Mrs Pulaska did nothing as she was carried into it, but merely stared at a horizon that was out of sight of the rest of us.

We followed my father across the farmyard and paused before the red door.

'She'll not need this anymore,' he said in the voice of a man finally proved right. He pushed the door open.

In the middle of the barn was a trestle table littered with implements – chisels, paintbrushes, metal files, a heavy hammer. Half-opened bags of plaster and tins of paint were scattered around the table legs. But it was the walls that had altered beyond all recognition.

On them were human figures, some of them painted and some built up in relief. All of them were naked. Skeins of barbed wire threaded across and through their bodies, and there was a subdued, ghostly glitter where the light caught tiny reflective fragments fixed in the vertical surfaces.

I was horrified and fascinated, and walked slowly round the walls. The more I stared, the more detailed and terrifying the work grew. Here was a face with stones for eyes and teeth of rusted metal. Here were children, their bodies splayed and dissected by hooks and claws. And here were tortured men with hearts of fractured tile, beaten women with skins of shattered glass. Ribs of animals protruded from their chests and the skulls of beasts showed beneath their faces. A hundred or more tiny bones had been set in plaster to resemble the shadow of an infant. One figure reached out, its fingernails delicately fashioned from filed portions of horn, but its face was a mere daub of paint in a white circle. These people had no dignity, no hope, and no escape. If ever I had any doubts about their fate, these walls would have told me what it had been.

I came back to the door. I was trembling and the smell of fire was in my nostrils.

'I don't understand this,' my father said.

Glowing flakes of soot drifted around us.

'It's a record,' I said.

He turned to my mother. 'I told you it would be worthless. The sooner we get rid of it, the better.'

He walked to the table and picked up the hammer.

My mother took him by the arm. I could see the force in her grip.

'Don't you dare,' she said.

Nitrate

OLD FILM IS perishable and mutable, able to transform itself into liquid or powder or even to ignite spontaneously. The safety film archive is housed in air-conditioned vaults, but nitrate films are stored in refrigerated bunkers beneath water tanks that will empty and flood the racking if fire breaks out.

I have worked for the institute for twenty years and I am known across the world. Film historians, archivists and restorers seek my experience and advice. My name appears on the end credits of more than two dozen documentary compilations and in the acknowledgements of over thirty publications on the birth of cinema. I am a success, but I seldom talk about my work to my wife.

She knows, of course, that I spend my working life salvaging ancient images and writing the occasional scholarly monograph about subjects in which she has scant interest. In the early days, when I restored footage of the 1898 Boat Race and the 1900 Lord Mayor's Show, she could see the point in what I was doing. Suzie appreciates pageantry, history, ritual; they offset her sense of fiscal prudence. Latterly, however, I have specialised in the work of pioneers who shot amateur dramas in their back gardens and developed the film in their kitchens. I have preserved short reels by Cecil Hepworth, R W Paul and other film makers whose identities will always remain unclear to us.

My wife regards such films as flippant and expendable, and she believes that preserving them is a waste of resources. For about two years I have not asked Suzie a serious question about her own work, and she has not asked one about mine. The smoothness of cliché is currency enough for us – *several tax clients phoned*, or *it was a quiet day today*, or a comment about driving conditions or the weather or what we each ate for lunch.

Perhaps that awareness of drifting apart also makes us keep our physical distance. Or perhaps it was mere familiarity, and its attendant twin of boredom, that led us into a separation from each other.

Suzie is still an attractive woman: I can see that plainly. On film, expertly lit and on a big screen, her good looks would be even more evident. But I no longer have any physical interest in her and we have not shared the same bed for three years. It is even longer than that since we made love.

Letters and bundles of accounts arrive with Suzie's name on them. She picks them up from behind the door as I am about to leave. She looks through them and I see a change in her stance when she notices particular envelopes. As the image is important to me so is the written word to Suzie. Every day she gets mail, but I get very little. Only at the archives am I sought after.

Without asking any questions I close the door behind me. I do not know what time I will return. If I am working on a particular tricky or interesting section of film, I often stay at my bench until the security officers tell me they must lock up.

Before we married, Suzie and I worked in cities a hundred miles apart and wrote to each other every few days. Although we phoned as often as we could, there was something especially intimate about writing, and in particular handwriting. In those days I said things that must have been over-ardent and hyperbolic and that Suzie insisted were paralleled in the very shaping of my script. Although I did not suspect it at the time, many of those things turned out not to have been true.

She has kept my letters somewhere. I don't know where; but probably at the bottom of the upright metal cabinet in the room she uses as an office. Certainly her other personal files are locked away in there. I do not have access to her records, but I once stole a look at her keyring and made a note of the lock number. At the archive there are several cabinets from the same manufacturer. It was not difficult for me to obtain a key with an identical number to Suzie's.

And her letters to me?

Why, I burned them years ago.

When I reach the archives I check the morning's messages, answer some queries, and then visit the nitrate vaults. A particular stack of cans, recovered from the attic of an Edwardian house that was demolished two years ago, has interested me since it was donated to the institute. I have already restored several reels from the cans.

To modern sensibilities these recovered works are extremely naïve. There is no sense of the structure or ambition of Porter's *The Great Train Robbery* of 1903, and no awareness of the tracking camera that Nonguet and Hatot introduced into post-Meliès productions. Instead the films only last a few minutes, and almost inevitably the camera is fixed in position five feet from the ground and twenty feet from the subject. There are no close-ups, no pans, and no sense of montage; such arts were all being developed elsewhere.

Perhaps even more notably the narratives belong to a vanished age. Tales of loyal dogs, thieving vagabonds and ludicrous villains, and resourceful infants were the unquestioned storylines of popular newspapers and music hall sketches of the time. But the historical value and strange poignancy of the footage, with the performers long dead and the gardens vanished, become more potent with each passing year.

That evening Suzie asks what kind of film I'm working on.

I am taken aback and instantly suspicious. Why such a question now, after all this time?

When I demur she asks if I'm not pleased by her interest.

Her direct stare is a form of challenge. She has recently had her hair tinted so that when she turns I can see shining gradations of blonde, as if she has been professionally backlit.

I reply that I'm not quite sure what kind of film it is, because the can has not been labelled and there's nothing on the feed. I suggest it could be a sporting event or the record of a celebration or a festival, rather like the material that Mitchell and Kenyon filmed in the early 1900s. But I concede that the likelihood is that it will be a pleasant little drama from the days when seeing images move was novelty enough for any audience.

I do not tell Suzie the truth. I have already taken a magnifying glass to several frames and found a man spying on a woman standing in an Edwardian bathing costume outside a beach hut. A large towel is spread on the ground. The film is evidently a piece of titillation for gentlemen's clubs, a kind of *What The Butler Saw* which to modern tastes will seem either relatively or entirely innocuous, but still not the sort of find that my wife will consider viewing, let along salvaging.

'Why don't you know?' she asks. 'I mean, why don't you just project it and see?'

I have been through this before. I'm sure she has not forgotten. More likely she is deliberately making conversation. I do not know why.

'Because the heat from a projector bulb can make nitrate film burst into flames,' I tell her. 'The stock is dangerous; a kind of cousin to nitroglycerine. That's why we have to transfer nitrate to safety before anything can be properly shown. Originally projectors had a scissoring device to isolate a strip if it suddenly ignited. If it did flare up then the fire couldn't be stopped and that section of film was completely destroyed. All its images disappeared forever. If there had only been one copy, no one would ever find out what had been on it.'

Suzie nods as if she is only pretending to be concerned. I can tell that she feels she has done her duty, or possibly indulged me in a manner she thought I would appreciate.

'I'm invited to lunch next week,' she suddenly announces.

But Suzie is often invited out to lunch or dinner. She is a freelance tax adviser whose clients are sometimes grateful enough to buy her meals. Six or seven years ago I sometimes accompanied her. Not anymore. I had little in common with the people I was required to socialise with.

'That's good,' I reply, uninterested.

I am thinking of my work and its dangers. Sometimes there are small nitrate fires when reels are being examined at the workbenches. Combustion continues even when the strip is submerged. Noxious yellow smoke streams from the water surface; breathe in those fumes and they turn to acid in your lungs. Those outside the profession never think of an archivist as leading a potentially hazardous life.

'Why did you make a special point of telling me about a lunch invitation?' I ask after a short while.

'I did it because it could be important. Maybe I'll be offered a job. It's for an old friend, Steve Tiplady. Remember him?'

Suzie is so eager for me to acknowledge that she is being open and honest that I immediately suspect there are things she is not telling me.

'Tiplady? Didn't you once work with him?'

'Six or more years ago, yes. I reported to him, and sometimes we went to conferences together. Back in those days we did presentations on VAT returns for small businesses.'

'I remember the name. That's about all.'

'I had a message from him a couple of days ago. Steve works at a very high-powered accountancy firm now. He sent me the publicity material they hand out to prospective clients and wondered if we might discuss matters. So I rang him to say yes and he invited me to lunch.'

'I thought you were happy being freelance.'

'I am, but to some extent it depends too much on chance. Some part-time work for Steve's company would provide a reliable income. I'm attracted to that.'

'Yes,' I say after a little consideration, 'I can see why that would appeal.'

Sometimes one becomes an expert by chance. I have examined, authenticated, and preserved several dozen little dramas by now, and watched hundreds more. I recognise the beach hut. It is the same one used in a short diversion (one could hardy call it a comedy) in which an ardent young blade's pursuit of two virtuous sisters is ruined by the girls' dog, which runs off with the man's hat, harries him to play games, and so on. Despite the beach setting the film must have been shot in a studio open to daylight. The hut is a theatrical flat, the background of dunes evidently painted, and the sand is thinly scattered over an all-too-obvious floor.

Perhaps I recognise the performer, too. The girl in my new film is very similar to one of the virtuous sisters. She wears an identical horizontally-striped bathing costume, with a similar if not identical ribbon tied in a bow above her forehead. It fastens up curly hair which would, I guess, be auburn in colour. She is quite heavy-set and with wide hips and thighs – the kind of sturdy figure that was much admired in the early years of the last century.

My detective work is not as extraordinary as it may seem. Sets, furniture and props were often used several times in the early days of cinema. For instance, historians recognise a particular feathered hat that makes its appearance in at least four works made by Film d'Art in 1908, the most famous of which is *L'Assassinat du Duc de Guise.*

So while Suzie meets her old friend and talks about tax laws, old colleagues, and the chance of employment, I begin to get my new film, my little piece of voyeurism, into as good a shape as possible so that a viewable copy can be made.

Almost from the start I know that it can be saved. Always when I open a can of nitrate stock there is distinctive and unpleasant smell, like unwashed underwear. I learned a long time ago not to be alarmed by this. But occasionally I have found the contents turned into dust, and often the entire reel has melted into an unusable mass of what restorers call honey residue. And sometimes only a few random frames can be saved as prints. At such moments I always wish that somehow, somewhere, I would be able to locate a near-identical copy. It is always a forlorn hope.

Lying in its circular metal can the new film has a strangely organic look, as if it is the remains of something that was once alive. The surface is coated with grime and several of the frames have shrunk. Parts have become brittle and some loops have stuck together. Certain sections have crumbled badly at the sides, destroying the sprocket holes and eating into the edge of the emulsion.

Several frames have become detached within the reel; perhaps at its last projection the film tore and was never spliced. I take the separated frames from the can as a pathologist might lift an organ from a body and study it under a magnifier. Deep scratch marks run down the surfaces, the image appears unclear, but I can still bring the film back to life. The frames show the girl rolling down the top of her bathing suit so that her breasts are exposed.

'What happened?' I ask Suzie.

She looks at me, startled. 'What do you mean?'

'Did you get the offer of a job?'

It seems at last that she understands me.

'Oh, you mean from *Steve*. No. It didn't quite work out in the way that I'd hoped.'

'Oh?'

'No, well, you see, it turns out that Steve isn't happy working where he is. He sent me that brochure just as an illustration of the company structure. And his new manager is being very unhelpful. I didn't quite understand that when we talked on the phone.'

'Didn't he make it clear?'

'He can't have done.'

To me this sounds odd.

'So what's happening?' I ask. 'Nothing?'

'You're quite interested in my work all of a sudden, aren't you? I'm not used to this.'

'Don't tell me if you don't want to.'

'I don't mind. Something *is* happening. Steve's thinking of going it alone; that was always his ambition. In a way he's been working towards it for years, and his current difficulties have helped make up his mind. He says he has the contacts and that a lot of his existing clients will follow him.'

'So he's doing the same as you did, but maybe more successfully.'

'That was a hurtful comment.'

'I was just being honest. So what has this got to do with you?'

Even as I ask I know what the answer will be.

'He has asked if I would be interested in joining him when it happens.'

'As his employee?'

'As his partner.'

'I see.'

Now Suzie's speech becomes quick and slightly nervous.

'I'm quite honoured, really – and a little, well, touched. I knew Steve thought I was efficient, but I didn't realise how much he actually *appreciated* my work. We haven't discussed the details of any partnership but we'll have to do that soon. I think he expects to take the leading role. I've no objection to that because he has more experience than I have – and more contacts. So we'll have to have more meetings to try to sort everything out.'

'But you'll have to invest money into the arrangement.'

'He'll do the numbers on that and I'll check them.'

'You're considering leasing office space?'

For a second Suzie appears bemused, as if such a move has not occurred to her.

'Yes,' she says, 'yes of course we'll have to do that. Eventually.'

Later when she is taking a shower, I sidle into Suzie's office and open her desk diary. The lunch date is marked. A very large M has been carefully written, almost crafted, beside the time and place. I close the diary and look around. Her tall metal cabinet stands in the corner. I don't know why she feels she has to lock it.

A laptop is open on the desk. I turn the screen on and read the list of her incoming mail. There is an unopened one from Steve Tiplady; the heading is *Wonderful to meet again*. I turn away and leave the office.

On the next day I take a spare reel of safety film and scissor from it several short, narrow strips that contain usable sprocket holes. These I fix onto the nitrate film, replacing those that are torn or missing. It is a delicate, laborious, time-consuming process. The alignment has to be exact and each strip has to be held in place with nitrate cement, a clear liquid that reeks of acetone and has to be applied with a very fine brush.

A few days later, when all the damaged sprockets have been replaced, I splice together the broken ends of film. And then, wearing kid-skin gloves, I clean the film with a soft absorbent cloth. This also takes days to complete, but the time does not pass slowly. Prior to cleaning the images have been difficult to make out, but now I know that what I saw earlier was no piece of mere teasing. Instead of a disappointing and jokily anti-climactic end, the last section of film shows a brisk emotionless copulation taking place on the towel in front of the hut.

When I am confident that the footage can be left to rest I visit the institute's library to carry out some research. I consult catalogues, lists, histories and arrange special screenings in our private cinema: in my work a large screen is essential. Soon I am convinced that I have discovered the earliest extant film of a type that came into existence almost at the same time as cinema itself.

Within a few years of the very first films being shot,

men and women were engaging in energetic sex solely because of the presence of a movie camera. Because of that subject matter, little material has been preserved. The earliest surviving example is thought to be *La Bonne Auberge*, sometimes known as *A L'Ecu d'Or,* made in 1908. Some authorities believe that the Eugene Pirouls 1896 *Le Coucher de la Mariée* must have been pornographic, although only the first two minutes survive: these show a bride disrobing to her petticoat. .

I am certain that my own film belongs to a varied batch produced in England in 1905. I can imagine the sly complicity with which they would be distributed. Along with the entertainment reels for general exhibition a special reel for discerning customers would arrive. The film would be screened in a smoky room with only men present, each one noisily determined to prove himself a man of the world, each one secretly astonished and aroused. In both the explicit depiction of sex, and in the casual efficiency of the performers, the film would have been unsettling and audacious. Forget the staged idylls of family life; forget the silly dramas, the sporting events, the military parades. This shameless little act is more important. This is what really drives the world.

Before their transfer to a digital file many of the old nitrate reels have been copied onto cellulose acetate stock, but I am having my new film copied on polyester triacetate. Cellulose acetate breaks down too, with its own decay characteristic being a vinegary stench. Polyester triacetate, on the other hand is tough and virtually indestructible. This is the appropriate medium for my sequence of images. Why?

Why, because I am dealing in retrieved history here.

Suzie and Tiplady have begun to meet regularly. Sometimes they meet in the evening so that Steve need not take time away from his present employer, and often one of his friends, a solicitor, joins them to give advice. Usually my wife returns late. One night I sit up for her, but she tells me I need not have worried; it was just that the meeting went on longer than expected.

'You can come with me if you want,' she tells me blithely, 'but you'll be terribly bored if you do. Remember what happened last time.'

I shake my head and she explains.

'You didn't get on with Steve. Not at all.'

'No?'

'You said he was boring.'

'Did I?'

'Of course you did. I thought it was mean and spiteful of you to talk about my colleagues like that.'

But I'm not even certain that I remember Steve Tiplady. And many of Suzie's colleagues were invariably much too confident, slightly overbearing, and absorbed only by their own narrow interests.

I wonder if my wife has a photograph of Tiplady somewhere. There's probably an old one in her cabinet. If I could see it then perhaps I might remember him and put a face, and a body, to his name.

'Exactly when is this new partnership of yours likely to happen?' I ask later.

'There are still a few details to sort out. Nothing's straightforward, you know.'

Suzie is stripping lacquer from her nails. I am so familiar with the reek of acetone that I do not usually sense it, but this time it is so pungent that my eyes feel as though they are beginning to water.

'And I have to go on a short course,' she adds. 'It's only over a weekend. Steve thinks it would be a good idea.'

I can hear the hands move on the dial of the clock.

'What kind of course?'

'It's one for professionals running a small partnership – legal matters, insurance; things like that. It's supposed to be very good.'

'Don't you know all that anyway?'

'I know it for my own business. Working with another person is different. You have to have agreed protocols, decide responsibilities, sort out areas of decision-making and dispute; that sort of thing.'

'I see. You're both going on this course, are you?'

'It would be wise.'

'Together?'

'That would make more sense, wouldn't it?'

'Yes, I suppose it would,'

After a while I ask another question.

'Is it within easy travelling distance?'

'It's residential.'

'Where?'

'Oh, I don't know,' Suzie answers, affecting mild irritation, 'some coastal resort somewhere."

But I'm sure she knows the answer.

I think of the first time that Suzie and I made love, and I wonder if she and Tiplady will meet at the same resort. An autumn wind tasting of salt buffeted the seafront and rattled the windows of our cheap hotel as we lay together, our arms round each other. Suzie giggled and said that she wanted to make love in the open air, among the sand and marram grass to the north of the resort, but I said it would be too cold and beside, we might be disturbed. She coaxed me and made me promise that one day we would do that, but we never did. Three days after we returned home I took up my job at the institute.

The reel is being copied now. At this very moment it is being transferred onto stock that will last forever. The nitrate footage is being coated with perchloroethylene, which has an identical refractive index and will eliminate scratch marks by effectively filling them in. Inch by inch the drenched sock is being fed into a printer; frame by frame a stronger and immortal twin is being created. Drying boxes and fume extractors cradle the unspooled films at the far side of the printer. When the processes are completed the nitrate reel will be returned to storage, but the images on polyester triacetate will be available to anyone with a serious interest in the development of cinema, legal and social history, or human behaviour.

This is what they will see.

A young woman in an Edwardian bathing suit is stand-ing in front of a beach hut. A man, dressed as though he has been strolling on a promenade, peers at her from the top of a fake dune. She strikes poses that are meant to be coquettish, at the end of which she pulls down the top of her bathing suit. The man approaches with the exag-gerated walk of a music-hall Lothario. There is a certain amount of pretended coyness and extravagant gesturing between the two. The woman rolls the costume down to her ankles and steps naked from it. She has a surprisingly large patch of pubic hair. Then she lies down on the towel while the man strips off his trousers and shoes. He seems curiously embarrassed by his erection and contrives to hide it from the camera. They copulate quickly. The man's overlong shirt, which he has pulled up round his midriff, creeps down across his buttocks as he thrusts. Just as there is no foreplay, there is no languorous satiation afterwards. When he has finished the man stands up, picks up his trousers and shoes, and walks quickly off camera. The woman struggles awkwardly into a sitting position, her face suddenly averted. The film ends. The reel unspools. It has lasted less than three minutes.

The young woman is the performer who appeared as one of the virtuous sisters; the man is different. I am certain that I have seen him before, but I cannot recall in which film. I am aware that this uncertainty, this sense of being at the edge of remembering, will not let me rest until I finally discover the answer.

Suzie is away on her course with Tiplady. She has telephoned me. It was a short conversation, because although she was determined to be friendly and to put me at ease, I was equally determined to be unreachable.

I stand in her office with the duplicate key in my hand. I have rehearsed this moment for weeks. In case Suzie detects that her things have been tampered with, or suspects a break-in, I am making sure that I will not leave any fingerprints on either the cabinet or its contents. That is why I am wearing the kid gloves I use when cleaning film.

After several minutes delay, during which time I wonder again if I am doing the right thing, I open the cabinet. The click of the lock is metallic and ugly. I hesitate for several seconds before I slide open the drawers, pushing them back in again if I find nothing of interest. They rattle loudly on their runners and close with a crash.

I find what I want in the bottom drawer and squat down beside it.

Inside there are sheaves of paper, accountancy sheets, tax publications; a trove that must date back for years. Slipped edgeways down the inside of the drawer are envelopes that have been gathered into neat little bundles and tied with ribbon. I lift out a bundle as delicately as I lift frames from a film can. I do not recognise who the letters are from, but they are addressed to my wife. A paper wallet of photographs is inserted between them.

I lift out a second bundle. On these the stamps are very old, the envelopes quote my wife's maiden name, and the handwriting is my own. When I prise them slightly apart without undoing the ribbon I can detect faint smell of mould.

For a few moments I kneel on the floor with my old letters in my hand. Suzie and I had loved each other in those days, before we had drifted apart, before I began to devote all my energy and interests to the archives.

And I think of my newly-discovered film being printed, made permanent, fixed forever. It is all thanks to me, to my discovery, to my dedication. If I had thoughtlessly run the nitrate copy through a projector it could have burst into flame and been destroyed. No one would ever have seen it. No one.

I return to the first bundle of letters. The stamps are more recent. The topmost envelope was franked seven years ago; it was posted in a town only a short drive away from our home. I do not recognise the handwriting at all. When I lift the letters to my nostrils there is no smell of mould. They are completely dry.

I loosen the ribbon that binds them together.

Drowned

T HE LAKE WAS a dying invalid, shrinking within
high abandoned borders, losing life and mass by
the day. The hotel was now so far from the water's edge
that its rowing boats had been lined up unused beside the
empty car park. Rebecca opened the door onto a surge
of heat and walked across to inspect them. Sheep looked
up incuriously and then returned to tearing at the sparse
dry stalks of grass. The past weighed as heavily as the
air.

I took the suitcases from the boot and waited. No other
traffic passed; water supplies had become so critical that
the valley road was closed to everyone but the hotel guests.
Rebecca turned from the boats and studied the front of
the building.

'Has it changed!?' I asked.

'No,' she said, 'it looks just like it does in my dreams.'

I followed her inside and waited at Reception while the
bell tinkled in the back room. Hanging on the wall behind
the desk were photographs that had been taken before the
dam had been completed. The dates still visible, they had
been hanging in their wooden frames for almost a hundred

years. In all that time there had never been a drought as brutal as this.

The hotel owner came to greet us. I saw by the momentary change in his expression that he recognised Rebecca even though he did not acknowledge it, Instead he considered his records rather too fussily. The booking was in my name.

'You asked for Room Three.'

'Yes,' Rebecca answered. 'I've stayed in that room before. I think you remember me.'

'I do.'

'Room Three has the best view. I take it there's no problem.'

The owner's eyes flicked to me momentarily. 'Of course not, but you'll find the view has changed. The lake is almost out of sight now. They say it will rain tonight. Let's hope so.'

I looked more closely at the photographs. In those melancholy images long-dead villagers stared at the lens from houses, pathways and fields that had ceased to exist.

Rebecca grasped the room key like a talisman. I waited for her question. For years she had telephoned the hotel to ask the same thing. The answer was never what she wanted to hear.

'The man I was with: you never saw him again?'

The owner's unease was clear in the way that he shook his head quickly and decisively.

'No,' he answered. 'I'm sorry; no.'

As soon as we got to our room Rebecca waked around it in short, erratic, wandering steps. A floorboard creaked under her weight and she smiled as if recalling a secret pleasure. When she crossed to the open sash window and looked out I wondered how many hours she had waited there. I felt like an intruder but I knew I could not leave.

'Perhaps we should have scratched our names on the glass,' she murmured.

'You were too modern for fanciful vandalism,' I said drily, lifting the suitcases onto the bed. The mattress sighed as if embracing lovers had fallen on it.

She leaned forward against the window ledge.

'Sometimes I think it would have been right to do something like that: passionate declarations, impulsive actions, vivid fantasies – that's how our time was measured.'

I unzipped the cases. A sense of responsibility, almost of duty, lay within my head like an ache. Rebecca's taste for the romantic shielded a nature that was otherwise defence-less. I considered walking across the room and taking her in my arms.

'Maybe less dramatic gestures would have been prefer-able,' I suggested.

'Ones better suited to you and me, you mean?'

'Maybe: all I can do is form an opinion from what you choose to tell me.'

'This was your idea,' she said, still looking out. 'You were the one who said it might help.'

'We both hope that, don't we?'

I took out some of Rebecca's clothes and pictured myself running my fingers up the smooth skin at the back of her neck and lifting the hair so that I could kiss the nape. She had spoken of liking to be touched like this, but I had never done so. I was too wary of imitating Conor, whose habit it must have been. On their very last morning, hours before the argument that would separate them forever, he could have made that gesture. Although she had never told me, I could easily believe that a kiss on the nape of Rebecca's neck could have been the last declaration of tenderness between them.

She turned for the window and the moment broke around us.

'He's scared of water,' she said. 'He pretends not to be, but he is.'

I had no need to affect a particular interest: we both understood Rebecca's need for repetition.

'He can't swim a stroke,' she went on. 'He almost drowned as a child. That's why he never goes near deep water unless there's someone like me with him. And that's why he would never have rowed onto the lake on his own.'

I had long ago stopped remarking that the empty drifting boat had been enough to convince most people. Instead of replying I hung some clothes in the wardrobe – the same wardrobe that Rebecca and Conor must have used on their last holiday. They had dressed and undressed in the same room, made love on the same bed, looked at their reflections in the same mirror. Rebecca had told me that after Conor vanished she had stood with her face close to the glass, irrationally hoping that by some occult process she would see his reflection within it, look round, and find her lover magically returned. But the room had remained empty, and Conor had vanished forever.

She turned to the window again. The floorboard creaked as I crossed the room. I stood beside her, so close that we were touching, and looked out. The sunlight was intense and the heat seemed scarcely tolerable. A silted delta had appeared where the lake edge had been. I thought of water trickling from the upturned hand of a dying giant.

'He's still alive,' she said.

I did not answer.

'If I knew he was all right, that would be enough.'

'I understand.'

But of course Conor was dead. It didn't matter that no trace of him had ever been found. Everything he owned had been left behind, either at the hotel or at the house he had shared with Rebecca. Nothing had been removed. If he had wanted to escape he would have taken his passport, changed his bank account, packed some clothes. Despite what Rebecca believed, her lover had not hitch-hiked out of the valley in an existential attempt to forge a new identity. He would never be discovered elsewhere, labouring at a farm perhaps, his past expunged by catastrophic memory loss. No: whatever remained of Conor was somewhere in the lake, well beyond recovery now, his flesh stripped by pike and eels and freshwater shrimps, his bones scattered by the relentless lift and drag of the artificial tides controlled by the dam. I had heard his disappearance described so often that I had no difficulty in imagining it. Conor had been an impulsive, self-dramatizing man, easily capable of threatening suicide or murder. I could see him walking out into the rainstorm, his mind racing with fury and loathing. We are all attracted to what we most fear. He had been drawn to the lake, to the unattended rowing boat on the shoreline, to the misty rainy level where water and air fused together.

His decision had been insane and inescapable. He was a man driven to the immediate. To step over the side, perhaps with his pockets heavy with stones, would have seemed both necessary and just. To recover from that act was impossible. Flood-water bore him deep into the murky heart of the lake. Direction, light and breath withdrew like severed nerves. As his lungs filled and the last flickers of consciousness deserted his mind, the woman who would always love him ran in panic to search along the road. By then she had forgotten their quarrel; all she wanted was for Conor to be safe. But even as she searched he was being swept, rolled and dragged unseen between the submerged walls and destroyed houses of the drowned village.

'You don't have to come.'

'You might need me.'

'No,' Rebecca said, 'I won't need you. But come if you like.'

A path through dry turf ended in a ragged line. We stepped down onto a swathe of rough stones, sharp as road foundations, which had been deposited in a shallow ramp before the reservoir had begun to fill. Like barefoot children on pebbles we crossed it gingerly until we reached a plateau of bedrock. A strong gust of wind, generated by the heat, raced around us and then faded. Rebecca ran her fingers through her hair to untangle it. I imagined Conor reaching out to assist and kept my hands by my sides.

'Do you wish he was here?' I asked.

'I wish he could see all this. That's different.'

I could not resist a touch of mockery. 'Maybe he has. Maybe he's been back.'

'No. There must be reasons why Conor doesn't want me to know why he left or where he went. He'll stay away because he wouldn't want to take the chance of meeting me again.'

We looked at each other for a moment. I did not know what thoughts were running through Rebecca's head. Unexpectedly she reached out and took me by the hand.

'You know I have a better life with you than I ever had with him.'

She leaned further forward as if trying to make me believe. Sweat glistened in the hollow of her throat.

'He could never have given me the stability that you have,' she said.

It didn't seem much of a gift, but Rebecca was right. From our very first day together she had seen my talents as being for order, calm, and most of all support. That was what she told me she needed. She had never recognised that I would rather have given her passion, recklessness, and perhaps even danger.

Now we crossed an expanse of sediment that had dried into cracked plates curved upward at edges, as if they were the softened fragments of gigantic shells. Stalks of dead plants were scattered like runes along its edges. The landscape appeared as artificial as earth art.

'If it rains tonight,' I said, 'this walk will be impossible tomorrow.'

'A hundred years ago this must have been pasture,' Rebecca said. 'Cattle will have grazed here. Over there was the river where the villagers used to wash horses. There were willows along its bank. You saw the photographs at the hotel. Everything looked idyllic.'

But I thought that nothing back then would have been idyllic. Life would have been hard, constrained, and unvarying. Now all that remained of the river was a slug-gish ribbon, and all that was left of the trees was a series of black stumps, sawn off a foot or so above ground, their trunks corrugated by decay.

We stopped at a low broad rectangle of worked stone set into the bedrock. Within its boundary lay a solitary piece of white tile, no bigger than a thumbnail. We were standing beside what had once been a house.

I stepped across the foundations and bent to pick up the broken tile. The gaze was marked with a blue line that curved like the outline of a heart.

'Victorian?' I asked.

Rebecca nodded and walked on.

'Maybe I should keep it,' I said.

She did not answer. I hesitated a moment and then put the tile back where I had found it.

Now we came to mounds of pallid rubble, like spoil heaps, and a collapsed maze of stone walls that had marked out pathways and barns. The vestigial remains of one wall dipped below the unmoving surface of the reservoir, its upper stones protruding from the sunny water like the floats of drift nets. Submersion had scoured the rocks free of lichen so that they looked as new as on the first day of creation.

'We used to imagine a complete village,' Rebecca told me.

'But you must have known it would be something like this.'

'It's easy to fool yourselves when you're in love. We would drift in our little boat and pretend that everything beneath the water had been preserved untouched, and that if the reservoir emptied the houses would emerge as good as new. We imagined chimneys and rooflines breaking the surface. We pictured families walking back in amazement into the village, not knowing if it was real or they were dreaming. And then, when they knew it was true, bringing in furniture, lighting he fires, making all the buildings live again.'

But there was little of the demolished village that was recognisable. Building stones lay scattered across obliterated streets. After the houses had been emptied the doors and windows had been removed, the plumbing ripped out, the roofs stripped, the joists and beams dismantled, and then the walls had been razed as ruthlessly and efficiently as in a Roman victory. Within a few days of its abandonment the village would have resembled an archaeological site, a patterned wilderness of ruins, its design and function accessible only to those with a specialised knowledge of the past.

I stood looking around as Rebecca walked towards a line of stone mounds.

'There's nothing left to dream about,' I said. 'They even cut down the trees.'

She called back across the empty spaces, her voice as sharp as a line drawn on blank slate.

'This must have been the church. It was deconsecrated before they pulled it down.'

I followed her to the foundations. The rubble had been stacked in irregular cairns with fans and swirls of gravel around each base. It was so hot that our breathing became laboured.

'There are no dressed stones here,' Rebecca said. 'It's all infill.'

I picked up a piece of rock from the pile. Some of the stones had fallen inwards, as in a collapsed burial chamber. I had the sense of looking into a destroyed puzzle.

'And the bells, pews and font?' I asked, replacing the rock in exactly the same position.

'They went along with the coffins and headstones to the new village down the valley.'

I looked around but could see no sign of a graveyard. Gardens, grass, plants – everything fertile had been reduced to baked mud and rock. Fifty paces away the stream emptied into the lake without a ripple. The rotted carcass of a sheep lay nearby with its legs pointing towards the water.

'Everyone took what they could,' Rebecca said. 'These people didn't desert their past. They took their memories with them.'

Lost in thought she stood motionless among the debris, her shadow etched on the ground as sharply as a stencil. I turned away and walked to the water's edge. A few ribs had been tugged from the dead sheep and the track of a fox had been indented in the dried mud. One rib lay within the inert band of foam that marked the perimeter of the lake.

I glanced back at Rebecca. She had not moved. I was sure that within her memory she and Conor lay drifting in their gently rocking boat, the village out of sight below their keel. I took a few more steps along the littoral.

I imagined that the sheep had drowned weeks, maybe months ago but had been beached as the water levels had dropped. The matted fleece was collapsing through the ribcage and wool had peeled away from the skull. I walked slowly past the body, taking care not to step on the bones, but suddenly there was a grating crunch beneath my feet. When I lifted my boot I saw that I had stepped on a tiny bone that was half-hidden by mud. I walked on, but after a few steps turned back.

I stood beside my footprints and stared down. The bone shone a clear bright white in the tread pattern. I bent to examine it more closely. Heat pressed hard on my shoulders and neck. After a few seconds I reached down and pushed away the enclosing silt. It had the grainy texture of paste. The bone was small, complete, unbroken. I picked it up and turned it between thumb and fingers. Mud fell away from its surface. I stepped towards the lake edge.

The water was warm and slightly oily, as if given texture by dissolved fats. I rinsed the bone and placed it in my palm. In this light I could see every detail of my find. After a short while I laid the bone between the joints of one finger.

It was the same length.

I walked back to the razed church with my fist tightly closed. The weight and texture of the bone felt as familiar as a key. Rebecca was standing at the site of the altar. I could not disguise my expression.

'Have you found something?' she asked.

'It's nothing,' I lied, and quickly pointed towards the head of the valley with my free hand. Broad whorls of cloud had begun to form above the skyline. 'It's going to rain soon.'

'Not for a few hours yet.'

The bone was clasped so tightly in my fist that I could feel its impression on my own fingers.

'Do you want to stay here any longer?' I asked. 'Or is it all too disappointing?'

'I didn't realise how much I needed to see this. I'm pleased we could do it together.' And she suddenly laughed in amused bafflement. 'He was a bastard, you know. He really was. I didn't see that at the time but I see it now. And to go off like that; just to throw everything away. I can't understand why he did it.'

My mouth was dry. I ran my tongue across my lips and watched the cloud slowly rotate as if on a great invisible hinge.

'It must have been my fault,' Rebecca said at last.

'It can't have been your fault. None of it was. You can't take the blame for the kind of person Conor was.'

'But I can take the blame for making him leave,' she insisted. 'I must have said or done something that made him do that. And I have to carry that guilt. Wherever he is and whatever he's doing, he'll not be talking about me. Conor will have put the past behind him. He's that kind of person. I'm the only one who will talk about it. I'm the one who has to live with the memory.'

Until that moment I had not realised that just as Rebecca needed Conor to be alive, I had needed him dead.

'It wasn't your fault,' I replied patiently. 'Whether he walked away into another life or drowned in this lake it was his decision, not yours.'

'He has to be alive,' she said.

I did not answer. Instead I changed my grip on the bone and imagined eels eating the flesh from a human hand,

'I couldn't bear it if he was dead,' Rebecca continued. 'I couldn't live with myself.'

Her face had the same fascinatingly haunted expression that I had seen when we had first met. I am always attracted by those who have been damaged. Sometimes I even see myself as a kind of saviour. I am secure being as I am; it characterises my life. And if there is a choice to be made, I always make the wisest.

'You'll always miss him, won't you?' I asked.

She did not answer for several seconds. When she did it was in a small, crushed voice. 'I don't ever want to see him again,' she said.

I walked back to the highest mound of stones and stood beside it. I was so tense that I felt myself sway. If I had looked down at my shadow I was sure I would fall.

'That's not an answer,' I said.

'You already have the answer. You have the answer every day that we're together. No one has ever known as much about me as you.'

I grasped the topmost stone and lifted it free. Its weight and shape were strangely satisfying. Beneath it a dark webbing of fissures led into the unseen centre of the mound.

'You rescued me,' Rebecca said.

'Yes,' I said, 'I know.'

I placed my free hand over the cairn and then gently tilted it towards the vertical. For a few seconds the tiny bone remained stuck to my palm, but then it fell from my skin and into a gap between the stones. There was the faintest of clicking noises and then all was silent. I replaced the stone on top of the mound, sealing the bone within it. The future settled around me; I recognised its architecture.

'What was that?'

I dusted my palms together. The shape of the bone was still impressed in one so I closed my fist tightly around it.

'Just an old piece of tile, I said. 'I was going to take it back but it doesn't seem right to leave it. I don't think anything should be taken away. Whatever was left here belongs here.'

It was true. Instead we would carry away, and never be able to put down, something that was intangible but which had defined us.

A gust of wind stripped dust from the ground and whirled it like pollen towards the lake.

'The rain won't be long,' I said.

We walked slowly back the way we had come, tracing footsteps that had marked the dried mud like the tracks of revenants. As we neared the hotel a few drops of rain fell but the ground absorbed them without a sign.

After we had gone to bed the wind strengthened and heavier rain began to fall. Gusts struck the window and skittered across the roof. Rebecca began to cry silently. I did not ask why. Water flooded the gutters and drummed on the slates. I turned and cradled Rebecca in my arms as the rain fell without cease.

After a while we began to make love. At first it was easy and trusting, but as we moved together in the darkness, sharing a bed that she had shared with Conor all those years ago, I was overtaken by a sense of melancholy. It seems that our actions were governed not by tenderness but by determination. We clung to each other in what we did not admit was a kind of striving. Both of us searched, Rebecca for what she had lost, I for what I had never had. Nothing would ever change this. Love could make no difference to our fate. Our other selves would always be just out of reach.

Later we were unable to sleep and lay in bed listening to the storm. After a while, wordlessly, we crossed to the window opened the curtains, and stood side by side in the half-light watching the rain. All that could be seen of the exposed floor of the reservoir was an area of darkness that was now so wet that it was beginning to show a faint trace of reflective light. We put our arms round each other's waists and inclined our heads together until they were touching. Rain coursed down the windowpanes. A cold dim light blurred and wavered across our naked bodies. It seemed that we were dissolving in water.

The Numbers

A SUN THE colour of paper edged above the farm and the wooded hill. He walked quickly because he understood that if he slowed he would become thoughtful, too nervous, and then lose confidence and turn back. Crows, shiny and black as blotches of spilled ink, strutted and clacked in the misty field, and at its far perimeter a low shape slid through the greyness and then vanished. Danny immediately recognised the russet brush and purposeful slink.

Mud webbed the dark farmyard and a heavy reek of cattle layered the still air. Near the farmhouse door a dark green Land Rover was partly illuminated by a light from the kitchen window. Two dogs, Border collies, ran up with vigorously wagging tails and dirty paws. He scratched their ears contentedly: they had made no judgement on him. Quite suddenly the door opened and his brother stood there, his back against the light.

'For God's sake,' his brother said: 'Danny, what are you doing here?'

'Martin, I saw a fox,' he answered quickly, as though that alone was the reason for his presence. 'It was in this field just now.'

'You didn't come all this way to tell me that,' Martin said, settling a cap on his head and closing the door behind him. Danny noticed that he had lowered his voice, as though he did not wish his wife to overhear. 'And where's your car? You haven't walked all this way, have you?' After a pause he added, with a touch of resignation: 'I can see that you have. It's just like you.'

'I couldn't sleep.'

'Listen, it's not right that you show up unexpectedly at this hour. It's not the kind of thing that rational people do. Understand?'

Danny looked at the ground and traced an arc across a cobblestone with the toe of his shoe. 'It could go for your chickens,' he explained. 'Take the Browning; we could find its earth and dig it out.'

'What are you here for? Forget the bloody fox and just tell me why you're here.'

'I try to help. You know I do.'

After a few seconds Martin sighed and pulled his cap further down on his forehead. Eager to be at work, the collies circled round the brothers' feet, nostrils raised, their breath condensing in the chill air.

'I know it's early,' Danny said, and the words resembled a plea. 'And I should have thought harder about things. But I didn't want to wake you up.' He paused, and added: 'Both of you, I mean.'

Even as he spoke the details of his last visit shifted uneasily in Danny's memory and he felt his confidence begin to fail. But Martin hadn't yet mentioned the gaffe, the perceived insult, so it was possible that Sarah had never told her husband about what she had been asked.

'We still have to get up at the same time as you and I used to get up,' Martin said. 'Farming hours never change. Ten, fifteen minutes earlier and we'd have been eating breakfast. But I don't suppose you've eaten breakfast, have you?'

Danny did not answer. His brother could easily make him feel ashamed.

Martin walked past and unlocked the Land Rover's back door. As soon as it was open the collies jumped inside. Danny could hear the gritty brush of their paws on the floor as they turned round and round before settling down.

'There must be something I can do,' Danny said. 'Give me some animal feed, or a spade, or a hammer and nails – anything. Just tell me what needs doing.'

Martin unlocked the driver's door, opened it a fraction, and paused. 'I can't think of anything that I'd want you to do,' he said flatly.

'Don't you trust me?'

'As I said, I can't think of anything,' Martin repeated without varying his tone. He climbed into the driver's seat but kept the door open.

'I tried to get office work but no one will take me,' Danny said.

'That's because of the mess you got into. Didn't that occur to you?' There was a pause, and Martin added: 'No, I don't suppose it did. You're not the brightest with numbers, are you? Not the world's best planner. Figures don't mean much.' He closed the door and wound down the window. 'I'm going to check the flock in the west field. They'll be lambing soon. I'll be back in twenty or thirty minutes.'

'I'll come with you,' Danny said eagerly, and added: 'We should look for that fox.'

Martin did not answer, but instead shook his head like man confronted once again by a problem he had never been able to solve. And then he started the engine and banged on the horn several times. In response an upstairs window opened fractionally and yellowish light glanced down into the farmyard. Danny did not dare raise his eyes.

'I've got my brother here,' Martin called, his voice like a herald's.

Danny could not hear an answer, but he saw the light withdraw and heard the click of the closing window.

'Sarah will fix you something to eat,' Martin told him. 'After that, it's best that you go back home. Understand?'

'Is she all right?' Danny asked, a little hesitantly.

'Of course: why shouldn't she be?'

'No reason. I was just asking.'

'She's fine,' Martin answered, and closed the door.

Danny watched the vehicle bump down the road, its tail lights fading into a mist whose upper layers were melting beneath the angled sunlight. And then he opened the farmhouse door.

He stood in a small whitewashed room that had once been an outhouse. It had double hooks with working clothes and hats, shelves stacked with tins and opened boxes, waterproof jackets and footwear, a gun and shells, a small dismantled engine thick with oil, gardening tools, bags of what he assumed must be some kind of grain, and a flagstone floor spotted with dried mud. A spider hung in a web across the bulb in the ceiling. It annoyed Danny that he should be accused of a lack of discipline by a brother who had such a disorganised room. The next door led to the modern kitchen and it had been left open so that he could smell hot food and feel the warmth. He pushed his hands through his hair, which was damp and which he had allowed to grow too long. His shoes were muddy and he wondered about taking them off and leaving them next to Martin and Sarah's boots and Wellingtons, but decided against it. It was possible Sarah would not be pleased to see him: she could even demand that he leave.

He called her name, at first quietly and then loudly when there was no response. He heard her shout a hello from somewhere upstairs; he was not sure where – maybe the bathroom.

'It's me – Danny,' he shouted, although he knew it was not necessary to announce his presence.

There was a pause of six seconds – he timed it – before she called back that she would come down in a few minutes. He unlaced his shoes in readiness but did not take them off.

When Sarah appeared in the kitchen he could see that her hair was still damp from the shower, and that the strands were curled up at their ends; she had dyed it blonde again since they had last met. She wore an old thin sweater and jeans that were ripped across one knee, but the sweater appeared to sit awkwardly on her body, as though parts were sticking to damp patches on her skin. Once again, he could see why his brother had married her.

'Don't tell me, you'd like something to eat,' she said drily.

'I don't expect you to make me anything,' he replied, trying to be considerate.

'You wouldn't be here if you didn't want to eat,' she

answered, opening the fridge. 'I can do eggs, bacon, fried tomatoes, and toast. I'm sorry but Martin has just finished the last of the sausages. And I can make more coffee.'

Danny kept his coat on but took off his shoes and walked into the kitchen. The tiled floor was pleasantly smooth. There was a hole in one sock that his big toe poked through: until that moment he had not noticed it, but now he realised how incongruous it must look.

'Martin didn't say he was expecting you,' Sarah said. She had switched the cooker on and was arranging food in a frying pan.

'He wasn't. I couldn't sleep.'

'Something on your conscience?'

Danny thought it best not to answer; not just yet, anyway. 'I offered to help but he didn't seem to want any,' he said. 'It's not like it was when we were kids together.'

'That was a long time ago. We're all different people now.'

He was not sure how to answer, and rather than leave a silence, Danny thought of the food he was about to eat and said; 'You're very kind.'

Her response was so quick he was not even sure that he had finished speaking.

'Yes,' she said, 'I am. In view of what you said to me last time.'

Danny looked down at the tiled floor. 'I picked things up wrong,' he murmured, although he was certain that other men would have responded in a similar way to Sarah's careless teasing.

'You needn't hint that it was somehow *my* fault,' she told him, as though she had read his thoughts. 'What I said was normal conversation: you're the one who took it to be something else. You get carried away by your imagination, don't you? It's not the first time it's got you into trouble.'

'Sorry,' he said weakly.

'Danny, let's get it straight. I'm married to your *brother*. We're very happy together. We intend to stay that way. So let that be an end to things.'

He looked up, ready to defend himself. 'It was when you suggested—'

'I said *an end*. We'll forget that it happened and never speak of it again. All right?'

'All right,' he agreed, and bowed his head so that she would not see his discomfort.

It was obvious now that Sarah must have remained silent and told Martin nothing. Danny felt both pathetically grateful and at the same time angry that he was morally in her debt.

'Sit down,' she instructed. Her voice had not softened.

Danny sat on the far side of a polished wooden table that stretched between them like a barrier, and he tucked his feet under the chair so that his bare big toe was out of Sarah's sight.

'How's my nephew?' he asked after a short pause.

'Andrew takes his finals in a couple of months. Everything's going well. He's confident. And when he comes back home he'll be going into partnership with us.' Sarah went on as if making a company announcement. 'He has a really good business brain and lots of ideas about taking the farm in a new direction.'

'A family business, then,' Danny said, but she did not react.

'You should have let Andrew advise you,' Sarah told him. 'If you were too proud to listen to your brother you should have listened to your nephew.'

But Danny believed it would have been absurd to take advice from a twenty-two-year-old. And besides, he felt nothing but contempt for academic theory, especially when it was concerned with the practical skills of accountancy, management, and farm practice.

Food sizzled and spat in the frying-pan and when the smell hit Danny his nose began to run. He had not eaten a cooked breakfast since the last time he was at the farm. He searched in a pocket for a handkerchief, realising as he did that the only one he had was dirty. Sarah pushed a box of tissues towards him.

'Sorry,' he said after blowing his nose noisily and then searching for a container to drop the tissue in. 'It's a cold,' he lied.

'There's a bin over there,' Sarah said, pointing, and once again he felt inadequate for not noticing. 'Mist never helps a cold,' she continued. 'And the farm has been built in the shadow of a hill. As soon as Andrew gets here we'll take a holiday to anywhere that's hot.'

'Martin and I always played on top of that hill when we were kids. Of course the trees weren't as tall then. We could climb the lower branches together. And I used to swear to Martin that I could see the sea.'

'I hope he didn't believe you. The sea's ten miles away. It must have been your imagination.'

'It seemed real to me.' Danny paused, and could not help but continue. 'In those days I thought we'd own this farm together for the rest of our lives.'

Sharpness returned to her voice. 'Don't bring that up again: Martin gave you a good price for your share. If you'd taken advice you'd still have most of that money.'

The kettle began to boil.

'Sarah,' he said with a kind of mild insistence, 'these buildings and those fields used to be my property.'

'Yours? Only half of them were, and you couldn't manage your share anyway. You don't have the sort of brain that Martin and Andrew have. The partnership would have been bankrupt if we hadn't bought you out.'

Sarah lifted the breakfast onto a large plate and put it in front of him along with a knife and fork.

'Danny,' she told him, 'farming's not an occupation for lazy people or daydreamers or people who can't understand elementary accountancy.'

The comment hit him like a slap. For a few moments he held the cutlery in an upright position, like a character in an animated film, and then he pressed the point of his knife into the fried egg so that bright yellow yolk spilled from it.

Once the food was in his mouth it was evident to Danny that he was generating too much saliva, so he reached across for another tissue. He felt foolish because he had become so clumsy. Maybe being misunderstood was a natural consequence of being gauche. And it was demeaning and unjust that all the valuable work he had done on the farm had never been given its true value, either morally of financially. Not only that, but his contributions were habitually dismissed with a guiltless ease.

'I could help,' he said, like a supplicant repeating an appeal.

'Martin doesn't want you to help. Not anymore.'

'I'm good at practical work. You and Martin don't think so, but I am. I've fixed guttering and fed the animals and dug ditches and delivered lambs.' He was not sure if he sounded eager or desperate. And then he added: 'It would help if I could earn some money.'

'Yes Danny, if the task is simple then your work is acceptable. But you nearly lost us some of those lambs. And you're no good at all if the work involves thinking ahead or seeing consequences. Deep inside, you know you're not.'

He nodded weakly as though he agreed to the wisdom of such an arrangement. This was how it was, Danny thought as he sank into self-pity: he had never been appreciated. Instead he was exploited, unrewarded, and often unable to make himself understood.

Sarah put a mug of coffee down in front of him. On its side there was a picture of a Victorian strongman lifting a gigantic weight. And then she spoke with an artificial brightness, as if she needed to close off any further discussion of the future.

'You look as if you're enjoying that breakfast,' she said, walking to the sink, 'you're nearly finished.'

It took a few seconds for Danny to answer.

'Yes,' he said, 'yes I am. Thanks.'

'I have things to do,' she said briskly, turning to the sink. 'When you're finished, maybe you could make your way back home.'

It was not a question, but Danny answered with a justification.

'I think it was just as well that I came here. I saw a fox

outside. He was very close to the buildings. Something needs to be done.'

Sarah did not answer but he noticed the momentary despairing shake of her head. She was standing at the sink and facing away from the table. Danny studied her back for a moment and noticed how her clothing was still sticking to it. He fantasised idly about peeling it from her skin. And then, unexpectedly, overwhelmingly, he was seized with a kind of desperate clarity.

He stood up and pushed back the chair so that its legs grated harshly on the floor. 'I'll be back in a second,' he said.

Everything was different.

Life changes, and from this moment on both past and future dissolve and Danny lives only in the present. And now he does not think, he merely acts, and when he does he feels as pure and as faultless as a rain-washed stone.

He goes to the outer room, picks the Browning shotgun from the wall, loads it, walks into the kitchen and discharges one barrel into Sarah's back. She is catapulted forward across the sink, her sweater punched with holes, and then she slides backwards and sprawls on the floor in a clatter of falling dishes. The room is still shuddering with the noise and smoky reek of the blast and her eyes swivel helplessly towards the ceiling. Danny walks across the tiled floor and looks down. Sarah's lips are moving but he doesn't know if she is actually saying something or if he has been momentarily deafened. He uses his free hand to stick a finger into his ears and waits until his hearing returns. Her words are distant, muted, like whispers from beyond a wall. He shoots the second barrel into her head and the blast disintegrates it.

Danny goes back to his seat, finishes eating his breakfast and drinking his coffee, and then returns to the outer room and puts his shoes back on. He is still annoyed that there is a hole in one sock. For a short while he rotates the shell cylinders in his hands, and then he breaks and reloads the Browning. Its metallic clicks are as reassuringly engineered as the tumblers of a safe. Then he puts two extra shells in his pocket and goes back outside to wait in the chill of the farmyard with the shotgun held in both hands and level across his hips. In the barn the cattle are lowing, but the mist is clearing and the rising sun is the colour of a communion wafer.

He cannot tell how long he waits, but as he is growing cold he never stops hoping that his brother will return soon. Eventually the Land Rover bounces back up the track and stops at the very spot where it had been parked. Martin opens the door. He looks puzzled and annoyed and unforgiving.

'I don't want you to shoot that fox,' he says. 'This is *my* farm. *I* take the decisions. So you can put the gun back where you found it.'

Danny fires one barrel and his brother is flung across the seat so that his body is bent backwards and half in, half out of the cab. The engine is still running and crows are rising in a racketing wave from their roosts. In the back of the Land Rover the terrified collies yelp and whirl in circles trying to escape. Martin slides forward, moving in a heavy, ungainly yet unstoppable manner as though his centre of gravity has shifted downwards. He comes to rest on the muddy cobblestones with one leg crooked beneath him and the other held straight out. His hands flutter ineffectually and he makes a strange noise, part exaggerated sigh and part bubbling hiss. Danny aims at his brother's chest, fires again, and Martin's clothing shreds. Then he takes the spares from his pocket, reloads, shoots the dogs, and pulls them out of the back. Their bodies smell of blood and wet fur.

Danny returns to the outer room, picks up a box of shells, and loads two. He does not check their specification and he does not count how many are in the box. Then he walks to the Land Rover, steps over his brother, props the shotgun against the passenger seat, and closes the door. When he sets off he hears a dragging thud as Martin's body slips to the cobblestones. He can still smell the dogs so he opens the window. Chill air courses like a balm into the interior. As he drives away he does not look for the fox.

For the next half hour Danny follows a haphazard course, only stopping to fire at anyone he considers a target. As though seeking help he waves down another driver and fires through the opened window. He shoots two men at a bus stop but cannot reload in time for the third, who runs away. A nurse whose face he knows, but not her name, is killed walking out of a shop. A postman falls to the ground with letters scattering from his grasp. A mother pushing a pram is shot dead but her baby is spared. Lastly he stops as he nears a young woman on a solitary run, but when he checks the ammunition he finds that there are only two shells left. He ignores her and drives away.

Danny does not know how many shots he has fired or how many people he has slaughtered. Numbers mean nothing to him, and neither do names or personalities. And only when he has reached the coast does he understand that this has always been his destination.

He leaves the Land Rover at the roadside with the door open. A path leads through grassy dunes to the shore and he follows it with the Browning still in his hand. In the weak sunlight his shadow is just visible as it passes like a ghost across trodden sand and scattered litter. From the road far behind him comes the distant penetrating wail of police sirens.

Danny reaches a broad pebbled beach that leads to a cloudy sea. The grey and brown stones crunch and grate under his weight and he sits down heavily above a contour left by the last high tide. The air has a thin vinegary smell, and he can see tiny flies covering a dead gull that has been washed up on a nearby strand of blackened seaweed.

He takes off his shoes and his socks, placing a sock into each shoe. One sock has to be folded carefully so that its hole is hidden on the inside. Then he reverses the Browning and pushes it into the shingle with its barrels pointing upwards. He looks ahead to an unclear horizon. The sea has retreated across dark sand and the distant water has the dulled sheen of corroding metal.

Danny crooks his right leg to so that his toe is near the trigger, but his movements are restricted and clumsy and unreliable so he rolls up his trouser leg and tries again. This time the clothing is tight against his flesh, like the inflated cuff on a blood pressure monitor, and he has to force his toe inwards before it can touch the guard. But the toe slips and the shotgun fires.

The blast flings him backwards and for several

deafened whirling seconds he does not understand that he is stretched out on the shingle like a castaway. For a while he stares at the grey indifferent retreating sky and then he struggles to sit up. There is a pain along the right side of his head like the touch of a hot iron and a clotting ferrous taste in his mouth that he thinks could be both blood and explosive.

His fingers are quivering and there are garbled shouts from somewhere behind him but he cannot tell what the words mean or how near are the people who are yelling them.

Danny lifts the shotgun, breaks it open, transfers the remaining shell to the barrel alongside his right leg, and closes it again. Then he pushes the stock back into the pebbles. The stones click against each other like celebratory ice in a glass. He forces the stock deeper until it is lodged securely. A breeze from the sea blows across him and ruffles his hair and he remembers that he had intended to have it cut.

He puts his mouth close to the muzzle, flinches, and wonders if his lips will blister with the heat. Then he takes his mouth away and tilts his head to check how close his right leg is to the guard. He bends the leg so that the toe is near to the trigger. It will be difficult to get it right but this time he is confident he will succeed.

After all, Danny thinks, everyone deserves a second chance.

The Parable of the Waiter

H ISTORY TELLS US something of what happened. The
shooting took place at L'Hippodrome restaurant at
approximately nine in the evening of Sunday 17th February
1901. There is no dispute as to who fired, but recollections
of the event are contradictory and the records of the Paris
police are incomplete. The official version omits the names
of two of the diners as well as most of what especially
fascinates us about the case.

At the time, the events of that night were chaotic and
senseless. After far more than a century, our knowledge
of history gives us some objectivity. Those who saw the
shooting felt only a baffling immediacy; it is we who are
able to supply meaning. A modern perspective is based on
the achievements of the most important person in the story,
although he was not present to witness what happened.
He was far away in another country. And yet without him
the shooting would have been just another gesture: histrionic, foolish, fatal, and forgotten. It was, after all, an age
of destructive gestures.

Afterwards he had to imagine the scene from details
supplied by those who had attended that farewell dinner.

But he did not ask the waiter what had happened, and the waiter saw it all. The waiter took the order, served the drinks, and was ordered to clean up afterwards. We need not give his name because his name is lost to history, and yet everyone knows the name of the man who was not there.

The waiter must have had no reason to expect anything dramatic. Although it was only his second week at tables after months of washing dishes, it is reasonable to assume that he had already developed an ear for accents. It would have been evident that the five men in the group were Spanish; he might have recognised Catalan inflections. Waiters quickly become sensitive to the trappings of origin and class, so he could even have registered that one of the men wore a suit of green velvet that was much more ostentatious than the cheaper clothing worn by the others. The women were all French, and these he would have categorised immediately, although he may not have thought of them as models.

The waiter's concentration was fixed on a job he was still learning, but nevertheless he was aware that emotions ran high around that table. The forced conversation, self-conscious laughter and staged embraces were evidently part of a farewell celebration for the lean and excitable young Catalan in the green velvet suit. When this man stood up to make a speech the waiter did not expect it to be in French, but he anticipated that it would be indistinguishable from other sentimental goodbyes he had heard. As he spoke, the Catalan rested one hand on the back of his empty chair. It was the very same posture that the waiter had been asked to take while posing for a studio photograph the previous week.

Later the waiter decided that there had been something disturbing about the Catalan's intensity. The truth was that he noticed nothing unusual until the man pulled a number of letters from his pocket with a theatrical flourish. Then, bizarrely, the woman in the next seat dropped to the floor and scrambled away as if she were crawling through an invisible tunnel. The Catalan hurled his letters across the table and reached into his other pocket. This time he pulled out a pistol.

At this moment everything assumed a puzzling, dream-like quality. The waiter was unable to name the sensation until some months later, when he visited a cinema and saw a fantasy film by Méliès, now lost. Watching the film he understood that what he had experienced bore an affinity to slow motion.

The crawling woman reached the far side of her table and hid behind the chair of a man wearing a suit of scuffed black corduroy. All the time, the Catalan tracked her with the pistol barrel quivering in his hand. The waiter took several uneven steps backward until he collided with another table. He felt behind him until he was able to grasp its edge. It had a smooth solidity that was somehow reassuring.

Now, in an action that the waiter judged foolhardy but that he would later describe as brave, the man in black corduroy reached out for the gun and knocked the barrel to one side. At exactly the same time, the Catalan shouted *'Voilà pour toi!'* and pulled the trigger.

There was a flash that hurt the eyes and a noise that dulled the ears. If there was a scream, the explosion dead-ened it. The man in black corduroy held his hands up to his face and the woman shrank to the floor behind him. Some customers stumbled from their tables and ran in panic from the restaurant, knocking over chairs as they fled. Cutlery and plates clattered on the floor. A man began yelling as if from a distant room.

The Catalan's eyes were as impenetrable as shining glass. He turned the pistol and pressed it against his right temple. The waiter could see the skin yield beneath the pressure. '*Et voilà pour moi!*' the man exclaimed. And he pulled the trigger again. Momentarily lit by the flash, his face contorted brutally as the bullet entered his skull, and then the muscles relaxed and he toppled forward over the empty chair. Blood pumped fiercely from his wound. The air stank of burning.

In the shocked aftermath the waiter found himself abstractedly puzzling over the mechanisms of killing. The only deaths he had ever seen had been the butchery of helpless animals. This death was different. As in Grand Guignol, it was stylised, didactic, fabricated. The Catalan's body had even fallen over the chair like a discarded dummy. Only the blood seemed real.

Curiously, the waiter felt even less involved in what happened afterwards.

Like a creature in a dumb show, the woman picked herself up from the floor and embraced the man in black corduroy. He indicated his wrist and then his eye, as though he had only suffered minor damage. She was unharmed. Two of their fellow diners hurried out quickly as if to avoid contamination. Any customers who had remained sat in a profound silence or wept convulsively. The dying Catalan lay unmoving in his slightly absurd posture across the chair back. Blood had spurted across the green velvet suit and the scattered letters and was fading into the tablecloth.

Uniformed police entered the restaurant and customers began to talk again, volubly and noisily. One of the police examined the body and declared the Catalan still alive, so his motionless body was picked up and carried quickly out of the building. Some others from his table followed in a ragged, trembling procession.

The restaurant was full of diners who could no longer eat, with half-finished meals on the tables and cutlery littering the floor. The waiter thought vaguely about all the ruined food that would have to be thrown into bins. He looked around for guidance from his more experienced colleagues. No one knew what to do. The manager, who had been sheltering behind a door, appeared and took agitated, blustering control. The customers could not be kept waiting, he insisted, although it was evident that no one wished to eat. And the blood and the mess should be cleared up immediately: *immediately*.

Later that evening the waiter woke his parents to tell them what had happened. He reported it all with the startled relish appropriate to a crime of passion, but he needed the next day's newspapers to fill out more detail.

The dying gunman was taken to Dajou's pharmacy for first aid, but his case had been hopeless. He was moved to the Hôpital Bichot where, two and a half hours after pulling the trigger, he died. The newspaper gave his name as Carles Casagemas, and his profession as painter. The woman he had intended to murder was a Parisian housewife, Germaine Gargallo, whose husband had not been present. The man who had shielded her was also a painter,

Manuel Pallarés. Another Catalan, the sculptor Manuel, or Manolo, Hugué, was recorded as being present, as was Germaine's sister, Antoinette Fornerod. All these people were said to be friends. The report did not mention two other Spaniards, the collector Alexandre Riera and the critic Frederic Pujulà i Vallès, who had fled to avoid association with the suicide. Naturally, neither did it mention the man who was not there.

The waiter was content with the press report. He believed the motive of the shooting was clear enough. Casagemas must have been the jealous lover, Germaine the woman who had betrayed him, perhaps with the man Pallarés. That, the waiter decided, was as much as he would ever find out - as much, perhaps, as he wanted to find out.

The waiter did not know it, for the killing had made him feel thrillingly alive, but by the time he read the newspaper he himself had already begun to fade from history.

Like others named in this account, Casagemas has been absorbed into biography not because of his own qualities, but because of the achievements of the man who had not been there to watch him die.

Picasso was in Madrid when he heard the news. His reactions have not been recorded, but we may conjecture that he was engulfed by contradictory emotions of shock, anguish, guilt and release. Casagemas, once his closest friend, had become increasingly self-dramatizing and unstable, and yet less than a year ago he, Picasso and Pallarés had been so united in ambition that they felt themselves to be blood brothers. When they had quit Barcelona for Paris in the previous autumn, all three had arrived in the city wearing identical black corduroy suits.

At 49 rue Gabrielle in Montmartre these young men shared ambition, penury and a scarcely furnished hovel. It was here, in one squalid room with little comfort and less privacy, that Casagemas slept with Germaine, Pallarés slept with Antoinette and Picasso slept with a third woman, Louise Lenoir, known as Odette. So close were they, and so narrow was the space they shared, that Pallarés wrote out a half-joking, half-solemn list that showed the times that they would eat and paint and fuck, and fixed it to the wall.

For Casagemas this had been an existence that was almost religious in its agony. Unlike his friends he was unused to the ways of the street and the brothel. He was cosseted, sickly and addicted to morphine. By nature he was probably homosexual but unable to acknowledge it. With Germaine he was undoubtedly impotent. With such burdens, how could he not be in thrall to the transforming ideals of romance?

The others scoffed at his intensity, for the rue Gabrielle was a place where higher feelings were reserved exclusively for art. Casagemas rapidly angered the sexually uninhibited Germaine. His protestations and declarations verged on hysteria, and his obsession with suicide was both absurd and frightening. She was not alone in wishing her hopeless, infuriating lover go back to Spain.

Picasso recognised that his best friend had plunged into an erotic delirium from which he was unable to surface. A return to his rich and loving family seemed to be the only means by which Casagemas could be forced into self-realisation and recovery. So it was that, still wearing their black corduroy suits, the two young Catalans took the train back to Barcelona in the middle of December 1900, just as an age was ending.

But Casagemas was now so wedded to the histrionic that he could not simply leave and never go back. He vowed to return and wed the already-married woman he had, without her agreement, begun to call his fiancée. Predictably, Germaine wished that this embarrassing failure would never come back. Besides, she was already intrigued by Manolo Hugué. But just in case, and perhaps sensing a disaster of some kind, she was astute enough to return temporarily to the husband she had so recently deserted for the bohemian life.

Two months later Casagemas did indeed return, resplendent in a new green velvet suit, and this time he carried a pistol in his pocket. He did not stay at the rue Gabrielle, but at the apartment his old friend Pallarés had recently moved into on the Boulevard de Clichy. It was here, in conversation with Pallarés, that Casagemas finally began to understand the truth of his rejection and the extinction of his hope. Everyone should meet the next day at L'Hippodrome, he suggested. It would be a farewell party.

Casagemas was never to know that Germaine would take Manolo as a lover, or that within a few short months, he too would be replaced. For in May of that year Picasso would come back to Paris, more than ever determined to succeed; determined, too, to make sense and art from a suicide he had not witnessed.

So, in the room where Casagemas had spent his last night, a short distance away from the place where he had turned the pistol on himself, Picasso lay in the arms of his dead friend's mistress. And it was in this apartment, from July onwards, that he began to execute a series of paintings in which that troubling, volatile friend would reach an apotheosis.

Picasso had depicted Casagemas before, but usually in sketches, and from the left. Now he began to paint him in oils, and the side of the face that fascinated him was the side into which the bullet entered.

There are two versions of *Head of the Dead Casagemas*. One shows the corpse stretched out on a bed, its decaying flesh a vivid green, a bright candle burning alongside the head. In recognition of the cause of the suicide, the wick and flame are a visual pun on an aroused vagina. In the other image Casagemas appears to be standing, but his eyes remain closed so that he looks like a slain man unable to rest. In both paintings the scorched entry wound is clearly visible on the right temple.

There are further works - two versions of Casagemas in his coffin and, later and less successfully, *The Burial of Casagemas* and *The Mourners*. The latter paintings are crowded allegories showing figures gathered around the corpse in its shroud. Art historians lay particular emphasis on their palette, because these canvases mark the start of the blue period. This is the beginning of Picasso's domination of 20th-century art.

Within two years of the suicide, the waiter from L'Hippodrome had met the woman he would eventually marry. At the same time, Picasso was at work on *La Vie*. As if in an unexplained ritual, a near-naked Casagemas is embraced by a wholly nude Germaine while ethereal blue light saturates both their bodies and the landscape. In the same year Picasso sketched his dead friend again, fully naked this time, as frail and vulnerable as a virgin sacrifice, his hands shielding his genitals as in a Renaissance depiction of a body brought down from a cross.

Picasso never fully exorcised Casagemas, nor did he wish to. The act of suicide was much too fertile to be erased. It is probable that he also realised that, in a clear place beneath the turmoil of his imagination, Casagemas would have known that only his extraordinarily gifted friend would be able to fashion art and universality from such a death.

And did Picasso give Casagemas immortality? Of course not; only a god could grant that. What he did instead was to articulate an eternal remembrance. Picasso had the arrogance of genius. He knew that as long as there is art, then his work, and the death of one man, would be inseparable from its history.

Seventy years after he finished *La Vie*, Picasso died in the south of France. He was ninety-one years old. No other artist had been so famous, so prolific, so admired and so pilloried, so recognisable and so rich. The value of his estate was so huge it became a matter of guesswork; already his possessions, letters, photographs were being reverentially preserved. After his death, prices for his art continued to outstrip those of any other 20th-century painter. At an auction in May 2004, a winning bid of $93 million secured a canvas painted just two years later than *La Vie*. Recently his 1901 *La Gommeuse* sold for $67 million, his 1905 *Garçon à la pipe* for $104 million and his 1932 *Femme à la Montre* for $139 million. The highest price yet paid for a Picasso is $179 million for his 1932 *Les Femmes d'Alger*.

Neither the waiter nor his family were to know of such an ascent or such wealth. They had long been wiped off the face of the earth.

In his life the waiter did not see a single painting by Picasso. He would not have appreciated it if he had. For him, art was trivial. Almost anything else that went on in the world was more important.

What fascinated the waiter was history. Even as a dish-washer he had been aware that history could organise and clarify the confusions of both the past and the present. He was eager for guidance. When he was waiting at tables he saved a little money each week until he was finally able to buy a three-volume set of illustrated books that detailed France's imperial heritage. He read them closely, not miss-ing a single word, and then he read them again.

In the coming years he would often refer to these books. They were vital to his growing belief in destiny. Now the waiter clearly understood that he lived in a country that was the envy of the world. It had a character and vitality that was superior to any other, but what drove the nation forward were the needs and tastes of ordinary men and women. Art was irrelevant to their lives. What mattered was the everyday. His wife and son, the wages he took home, the rent he paid for their apartment, even an abstract idea like the good of the country, all were charged with an energy that lay outside the ambition of the squalid dreamers and their camp followers to whom he served food. Those people were too ignorant to share the common currency of patriotism, too obsessed with each other to be able to march bravely into the future. Art was ephemeral and histrionic.

In fact, art was just like the life of the madman who had killed himself close to where the waiter had once stood, pressed up against one of the tables he had been serving, in the restaurant where he still worked.

As the years passed, the waiter grew certain that the suicide had been forgotten. Perhaps those who had actually witnessed it would remember, but for those who had merely read about it in the newspaper the name Casagemas would have meant nothing. The waiter also reasoned that the dead man's life must have been miserable, hopeless and utterly unlike his own, which he assumed would be long, uneventful and characterised by honour and service. The waiter respected what God had given him. He had never contemplated taking his own life. Like thousands of his countrymen, he was, however, willing to risk its sacrifice.

Fifteen years after the death of Casagemas, the waiter found himself in military uniform. Near to his country's ruptured border he became part of a prolonged, massive, bloody and tactically pointless battle, which he did not survive. After a short while he did not expect to. No one's life was guaranteed. Time itself seemed to collapse or expand in a way that only had an analogue in fantasy films such as those by Méliès that he had seen in his youth. The shattered trees, the shelled ground, the smashed fortifications made up a landscape on which murderously imbecilic struggles were fought. All around were varieties of death for which Casagemas's orchestrated suicide could never have prepared him. Eviscerated bodies of men and horses littered the ground. The air reeked of mud, decay, shit and smoke. Explosions hurled earth, timber, brick, helmets and human limbs into the air. Everything was taken apart, time after time, and there was nothing fixed that a man could hold on to.

Partly deafened, filthy with lice and foot rot, the waiter hunched in a muddy shell hole and comforted himself by thinking of better times. Sometimes he conjured imaginary scenes of an Arcadia that would follow the war. Sometimes he remembered simple domestic pleasures, recollections of an everyday happiness about which the mysterious suicide must only have been able to dream.

Like thousands of others, he took a photograph from his tunic, held it like a sacrament in his hands, and stared at the faces of his wife and son. The waiter feared what would happen to them if he were killed, but his imagination was unable to foretell their actual fate. All he could imagine was that at the moment he was looking at their faces, perhaps they were studying a photograph of him. He could not know that soon a photograph was all that would exist.

After months of squalor and terror the end came rapidly when a shell burst just a few metres away. As the shrapnel entered the waiter's brain and he fell forward in his own silence and darkness, he felt a curious sense of justification. It lapped at the edge of his fading consciousness like an ocean on black sand. In that last moment he was astonished to find himself picturing not his wife, not his son, but the long-ago suicide of an unknown painter. The waiter understood that this was the last time that event would ever be recalled, but that his own sacrifice would always be remembered. And then his consciousness collapsed in on itself.

The waiter's family was erased from history in the influenza pandemic that followed the war. They died within hours of each other, and they shared a grave that was identified only by a number.

The waiter's body sank within ooze and gravel, the soil packing tightly over it. His flesh decayed, the buried helmet rusted, the family photograph faded and then shredded into pulp. The waiter was lost forever beneath earth, and then grass, and then saplings.

He had no marker. There was no known date of death. He did not even have an identity. He was lost within the guesswork of battle deaths as his family was lost among the guesswork of disease mortality.

The landlord made sure that the contents of their apartment were sold to settle debts that were due from waiter's family. However, since he often tried to impress his mistress with the breadth of his interests, the landlord gave her the three books the waiter had bought with his savings. Meanwhile, the apartment was cleared. Beds and furniture went without history to their next owners. Documents and letters were burned. The personalities of the waiter, his wife, his son all vanished. A generalised remembrance of the multitudes of the dead moved on through the lives of people they had never met and whose names they had never known.

Some weeks later, as she was getting ready to desert the landlord without telling him, his mistress leafed through the three books on history. She was not interested in what they had to say, but intended to sell them. A photograph fell from between the pages of one. It showed an ordinary-looking man posing awkwardly in his best suit, his face stiffened self-consciously and his eyes glassy with nervousness. His hand was resting on the back of a chair.

The landlord's mistress thought that the books could be of some small value, but a stranger's portrait was worth nothing. And if she were leaving she would have to go soon and never look back. Her love for the landlord was already in the past.

She tore the photograph in half and threw the pieces in a bin with the remains of a meal she had been too nervous to finish.

Giacomo's Juliet

I T WAS A day's drive north along the spine of England, and after I left the motorway I saw little but bleak hillsides and stone walls strung in lines across darkening fields. At nightfall a full moon rose and I slid the heater controls higher. Even then I did not want to take off my coat. Grit and salt had been scattered on the road to prevent icing: tyres had marked the surface as if sleds had been driven along it. I was relieved when the car breasted a hill and I was able to see a cloudy oval of light a mile of so ahead. It was my home town.

Everything was bright as I drove down the main street. Shop windows shone with colour, and near to my old school a creamy glow of floodlight washed across the façade of the new ice-rink.

My mother's home was on the far side of town, where the street lights ended and the houses gave way to hawthorn and rough pasture. When I finally drew up outside the gate and stepped from the car's muggy interior I momentarily reeled because the frost was so sharp.

I looked round as I searched for my key. Fifty yards away people were skating on a shallow pond. As a boy I had never owned skates, and on the few occasions that the pond had frozen over I had slid across it in boots. Now everyone could visit the rink, and owning skates was no longer unusual. I could hear the hiss and rasp as the skaters sailed and turned across the moonlit ice.

My mother was expecting me, but to reassure her I pressed the bell before unlocking the door. As I stepped into the hallway she was already on her way to meet me. We embraced, wholeheartedly on her part, uncomfortably on mine.

I had last seen her only a few months ago, and yet now she seemed more fragile and more distant. I wondered if my father's death and her new solitude were finally beginning to tell on her.

At the funeral she had refused the tranquillisers offered by her doctor; she had insisted that she wanted as clear a mind as possible. She was dignified throughout both the service and the short committal at the local crematorium, her composure only fracturing slightly when the curtains closed with a swish and one of my father's favourite songs filled the room. Even then she did not weep, but dabbed discreetly at her eyes with a tiny handkerchief. Afterwards she was clear-thinking, sociable, and apparently more concerned about the welfare of others than about her own.

When we said goodbye I suggested she should fill her life with new interests and perhaps new friends. I had thought vaguely of some kind of deeper involvement in small-town life. Instead she told me she was ordering a book on twentieth century sculpture. She had, she said, forgotten too much about contemporary art. I did not protest because I did not think her serious.

Now my mother's fortitude was less evident. I studied her surreptitiously as we sat opposite each other and ate the meal she had cooked. It was food I used to enjoy as a young man but which I now found less appealing.

Our conversation grew awkward and then limped into silence. In that moment her eyes became unfocussed and I saw that her mind was drifting elsewhere. For what seemed like a minute she stared at the far corner of the room. I wondered if she had placed something special there, so I turned to look. There was only a waste-paper basket filled with the separated pages of a discarded newspaper. One page had been cut in half. I wondered if this also demonstrated an erosion of her sensibilities.

I was about to say something when, disconcertingly, her hands moved to her breasts as though she wished to caress them. Embarrassed, I cleared my throat noisily and her attention came back to me. She spoke is if nothing had happened.

'And what are my grandchildren doing now? It would have been good to see them.'

'They're in Italy with their mother. She sent me some photos. Would you like to see them?

I took the phone out of my pocket, found the photos, and passed it over with an instruction on how to see all the images. My mother stared at them and then passed the phone back to me.

'You've never been to Italy, have you?' she asked.

'Maybe I'll go; one of these days.'

'Your father and I travelled all across Italy. We were very young.'

I had heard this story many times and was a little weary

of it. 'Yes,' I said. 'One of your family photographs was taken there.'

There were two framed photographs on the sideboard. The earliest showed my parents, not long after they had married, standing with linked arms next to a fountain in in Rome. It had been taken by a friend they had lost contact with many years ago.

Eighteen months later, a few yards outside this very house, a new neighbour had taken the next photograph. My mother held me in her arms, my father stood beside us, and in the background the edge of the pond could be seen. I looked the same as any baby, with a tiny closed face emerging from a knitted wrapping of white wool.

Both photographs had absorbed me when I was growing up, as they seemed to fix both my ancestry and my identity.

'People used to say you were the image of me,' my mother said. 'Your father never complained. And your children—'

'Everyone says they look like their mother, not me.'

She nodded. After a short pause she spoke again. 'The Piazza Navona: that's where we were standing when we had that photo taken. We were in front of the Bernini *Four Rivers* fountain; you can see it in the background.'

I did not need to examine the Roman photograph to know that there was statuary and water in the background; I considered them of little importance. My mother's image, on the other hand, had often intrigued me. I could never imagine her acting a star-cross'd lover; the theatre seemed something alien to her personality. And yet, all those years ago, as she stood arm-in-arm with my father beside the fountain, she had chosen to wear the cape she had worn on stage as Juliet. Behind them sunlight caught a stream of falling water and turned it into a spray of ice.

My mother's evident attractiveness had not disturbed me but the confident, supple poise of her body had. Even at the age I was now, I was still uncomfortable with the knowledge that she had been a sensuous woman and that her love for my father must have been intensely physical.

'It was one long, glorious summer,' she went on. 'Of course we didn't know you were going to come along so soon. In those days I couldn't imagine myself as a mother, let alone a grandmother. And I haven't seen my grandchildren since the funeral. It's not right.'

I shifted awkwardly in my chair. 'But I don't get to see them much myself. My wife—'

'You were foolish about that,' she interrupted. 'You should have forgiven her."

'I don't think so.'

'I understood what she needed, even if you couldn't. She's a good woman at heart. Hers was a foolish indiscretion, that's all.'

'It was more than that,' I countered as patiently as I could. 'She's pregnant now. You'd have thought that she and her boyfriend . . .'

I let my sentence tail off. My mother's expression had altered; I had thought she had known.

'Perhaps if you'd been able to make her happier,' she said after a pause, and almost immediately shook her head. 'I'm sorry. I shouldn't say such things.'

'It doesn't matter,' I lied, hurt but not wanting to show it.

'We could all have gone to Italy,' she suggested with an absurd brightness.

I gave a laugh. There was no humour in it.

'If things had worked out between you, you could have taken us all,' she insisted.

'Perhaps, but it would be impossible now. And I thought you didn't want to go back there. You always said *never go back.*'

'I believed it when I said it. I was wrong.'

She was silent for a few seconds, and then she spoke again.

'It's too late now.'

Yes, I thought; it's too late. My children had ceased to be really mine. They were drawing away from me as if from a man standing alone on the borders of his own past.

I encouraged my mother to go to bed early, but she wanted to stay awake to be the last to retire. She had always done that during the final year of my father's illness; perhaps she still gained a certain comfort from performing the same rituals – the check on locked doors, closed windows, switched-off lights. I was insistent, however, and spoke to her as though she was no longer able to decide for herself.

When she had gone I sat quietly and wondered what to do. After a while I found that I was unconsciously copying her, for I was staring into the far corner just as she had done. Nothing had changed.

I stood up and began to pace around a room that had seemed large when I was young, but which now was small, cluttered, and unattractive.

There seemed to be a vast gulf between the woman on

the two photographs, the woman who had presided over her husband's funeral, and the person I had been talking to. I was convinced that my mother had become suddenly older than her years, that infirmity was invading her mind, and that her judgement was failing.

I paused at the sideboard. My children had sent her a postcard from their holidays. It lay picture-side down with its scrawled message about having a good time. When I turned it over I saw that the picture side contained four gaudy image of Rome – the Colosseum. The Trevi Fountain, the Spanish Steps, and the Piazza Navona. I propped up the card so that the picture faced outwards, and brooded on how she had apparently forgotten that she had received it.

My parents must have lived a strange, rootless life in Europe, almost a bohemian one, but after a few short years they had relinquished it all and returned home. They took up jobs teaching English and never again returned to acting, refusing even to perform in local amateur productions.

As a youth I had imagined that an elaborate scandal had driven them to seek refuge in this small town; perhaps my father had fallen hopelessly, madly in love with another woman, an artist or countess perhaps. Now that I was much older I believed that their decision must have been made purely from economic necessity.

When I finally went to bed I lay awake for an hour, I was too close to my own childhood. This was the room I had grown up in; for years I had even slept in this very bed.

Pale light marked out a rectangle of window behind the curtains. Eventually, despairing of being able to fall asleep, I got out of bed, pushed aside the curtain, and stared through the glass.

The moon was high, cold as metal, and the deserted pond sparkled eerily beneath the bright constellations. I stood looking at it for some minutes. Everything was still, as if time itself had ceased.

And then I saw my mother walking towards the pond. She was following a straight line across the hard ground, and she neither flinched nor faltered, but headed straight towards the ice. She was completely naked.

For several seconds I thought I must still be in bed and somehow asleep, and that what I saw must be nothing but a bizarre and disturbing dream. During those moments of uncertainty she took several more steps.

Hurriedly I pulled on my trousers and sweater, and shoes without socks, and ran downstairs. The front door had been left open onto the chill silence and there was a smell of camphor in the room. What I thought was a dressing-gown lay on the floor as if my mother had slipped it from her shoulders before she walked out into the night. I snatched it up and ran outside.

The ground was as hard as a lava bed and the night air took my breath. An icy richness inhabited everything.

My mother stood at the centre of the frozen pond, perfectly still and relaxed, as if she were being studied by someone unseen. Around her bare feet were the glassy whorls of blade-marks, and the chips of scattered ice had had refrozen so that they glittered and shone as it quartz dust had been strewn across the surface. I felt that the universe itself had suddenly condensed into one place, and that all of our past lives was mysteriously present.

I walked towards her across the ice. It creaked beneath my weight. Only then did I realise that I was carrying not a dressing-gown but a cloak, and that it reeked of mothballs. I draped it across my mother's shoulders and then attempted to wrap it around her. All the time I tried not to touch her skin.

She looked at me with the rapt eyes of a young woman. They shone will cool fire.

'Giacomo?' she asked.

I felt my heart become sluggish.

The spoke the name again: 'Giacomo?'

I shook my head. 'Come back inside,' I said. 'Come back home.'

I led her up the slope and back into the house, washed her feet and dried them, and then took her back to her bedroom.

She was speechless now, too far distant, lost within her own imaginings. She raised her hands obediently for me to slip her nightdress back on. I had never seen her naked before. I was embarrassed, angry, and ashamed, and tried my best not to look at her.

The curtains in her room were still open. I reached across to draw them, but stopped. From her bed my mother could look through her window and see the stars. I left her gazing at them and went downstairs.

I was numbed, trembling, and unsure what to think. I sat with my hands clasped in front of my face like a man at prayer. The smell of mothballs was still coating my fingers; my mother must have kept Juliet's cloak hidden for almost fifty years.

She could never have forecast her fate, I thought; on the

day that she and my father had posed in front of the sunlit fountain she had been full of youth and sensuality. A friend's unclear photograph had caught the shadow of that lost moment. I had a wistful sense that my mother had enjoyed a much more pleasurable life than I had ever experienced. In the vanished Roman sunlight she would have had no thoughts of solitude, age, or death. If somehow her future life had been demonstrated to her she would have thought it unbelievable that she should end her days in a place like this, drifting into reverie, spending money on luxuries she did not need, and now driven to an adolescent's sleepwalk.

I crossed the room to the bookshelf. I had never examined the gift she had promised herself and I was curious to see how much money she had wasted on it. The sculpture book was heavy, and printed on expensive paper. When I opened it I discovered that it had cost more than a hundred euros. Such extravagance was in itself a kind of proof.

I began to flick through the book. It was in Italian. Brief sections of text were followed by photographs that filled entire pages. Soon I came across a newspaper cutting that had been folded once and slipped between them. I picked it up to see the photographs it had obscured.

One was of an artist's studio. A dark-haired man in working denim leaned on a stepladder with a hammer in one hand. Beside him was something bulky that was covered by a heavy sheet. Light from high windows spilled across a floor that was strewn with chiselled debris. The man's sculptures were shown on the opposite page – female forms, in white marble, partly abstract, but with curves, length, clefts.

I opened the cutting.

It was an obituary notice that had been cut from that morning's newspaper. Written in the margin across the top and down the edge, in my mother's hand, was a quotation—

when he shall die

Take him and cut him out in little stars

I scarcely noticed the dead man's surname, only his first – Giacomo. There was a portrait. It was the same man. He stared at me from out of the past.

I could not hold my gaze. He looked too much like me.

At about that time a thick bank of cloud came up from the south and extended across the sky. By morning a thaw had begun that was accelerated by rain.

My mother came downstairs as though nothing was unusual; only the way she averted her yes convinced me that she could remember at least part of what had happened.

I have never been a courageous man and did not have the nerve to mention it, or to ask about the dead sculptor. Perhaps I was afraid of what she might tell me. Instead I acted as if nothing had changed. But it had, and I had begun to hate my mother and be jealous of her. And although I had often heard it said that often men marry women who resemble their own mothers, it was only at that moment that I began to believe that the saying might be true.

Perhaps my wife could have understood my mother better that I have ever done. Perhaps she would even have recognised her form in a piece of chiselled stone.

But what of the man who had stood linking my mother

in that Roman piazza and who, little more than a year later, had stood beside her as she cradled me in her arms – if he had still been alive, what would he have done when his wife was transported so desperately into her past? Would moonlight on a frozen pond have reminded him, too, of marble chippings littering a studio floor?

The Reckoning

O N T H E R O A D to the caves I finally understood how little time was left. For a few moments I could neither speak to Julia nor look at her, and I pretended that the hired car was taking all of my concentration. Sunlight flared across the windscreen. Two hundred metres ahead something dark and unrecognisable was lying on the road

It was not that my sister refused to consider matters – in fact, the opposite was true. Julia's profession was the measurement of time, actual and hypothetical, and she had been rigorous in applying the probabilities to her own case. An hour ago on the bridge at Ronda we had hunched together against unexpected rain, and as we stared down the gorge's steep walls she had repeated the figures. But numbers had never been as real to me as they were to her, and until this moment on the sunlit road I had never been able to imaginatively grasp their consequence.

But perhaps I had understood earlier without realising. In the lightless hour of the previous night I had woken shouting from a nightmare that I had refused to describe, but which Julia must have guessed had been about her. In the puzzle of sleep I had dreamed of my sister's face with bright reflections where her eyes should have been. I had reached out and scooped away the light so that it cascaded down her cheeks like water from shallow pools. Beneath it were dull circular objects that I did not at first recognise.

Julia was looking ahead, a map spread across her knees, her thin hand resting on the crinkled white line of the Ubrique road. The surrounding limestone mountains were assuming ever more sculpted forms, and beside the road the cliffs were undercut by small caves whose mouths were clogged by scrub and debris. The rain that had swept across the plateau had passed over and the air was clear and bright.

'There's something ahead,' Julia told me, although I was already braking. 'It will be dark by the time we leave,' she added thoughtfully.

'It's all right,' I said, seeing a dog full stretch on the road, 'we can stay another night in Ronda if we have to.'

'I don't like changing our schedule.'

'I know.'

I thought that the traffic was so light, and the afternoon sun so warm, that the animal was merely dozing on the road, its paws pointing towards us from beneath a relaxed body. As we drew closer I saw that instead of a head the dog had a pulpy mass of red covered in flies. I suddenly wanted to vomit.

'Someone should pick it up,' Julia complained angrily as I steered round the animal. 'It's a health hazard as well as a traffic hazard. People should dispose of dead things.'

Her words made us both fall silent.

Beyond the next village the way to the caves was by a hairpin on the left that I did not see.

'It's there,' Julia said excitedly as I drove past, and then she added petulantly 'You missed it', as though I had failed in my role as driver and companion. I turned and drove back to the junction.

'You see, we lost nothing,' I told her, although I knew my sister had timed the delay. She did not answer, but pushed her hand back through her hair in a motion that was almost boyish.

Immediately the road narrowed, climbed, and developed into a series of blind corners. To our left stretched an uneven plain of olive groves, rough pasture, and isolated buildings with pantile roofs. Around one bend we came across a flock of sheep driven by a solitary man tanned the colour of stained wood. I pulled into the edge of the road. Not changing his pace, the shepherd looked at us curiously as he passed.

'He can't imagine what we're doing here,' Julia said.

'I can't, either.'

'You agreed to this. You know how important it is.'

'That's right. And if I didn't, you keep telling me.'

A few hairpin kilometres farther and we came to an unsurfaced lay-by that had been blasted out of the hillside. Propped against a rock was a painted wooden sign indicating that the cave entrance was 200 metres up a path. We were surprised to find several cars, some of them also hired, all parked in a line.

It was my last chance, so I looked at the sky as though night was about to fall very quickly.

'We don't *have* to go,' I said.

'I want to see the calendars,' Julia insisted, reaching into the back seat for her walking pole. And then she added, with a wanly ironic smile, 'It would be foolish to wait until the next time I'm here.'

'Fine,' I said. Sometimes it was important to be honest, and sometimes it was important to act as if nothing would happen – as if, in a year's time, everything would be the same.

A stone path zigzagged up the side of the mountain. Its steps were rough and irregular, and each one seemed higher than the one beneath. I led the way, taking it easy so that Julia would not fall too far behind. At each step I heard her breath as she leaned on the pole. After a few minutes we came to an angle in the path where we could stand on a narrow rock platform, ostensibly to look across the valley and the mountains, but in reality to make sure that Julia did not overtax herself.

Her breathing steadied, and after a few moments we looked at each other. Her face was gaunt but still beautiful. Our childhood moved between us.

'Who would have thought it would come to this,' Julia said softly.

I did not answer.

'Do you remember the last time we visited caves? We were on holiday in Yorkshire with our parents. We must have been about eight and ten.'

'Of course I remember,' I said, indicating my wristwatch. 'We should press on.'

In Yorkshire there had been a walkway, guardrails, and electric lights hanging from a cable above the underground stream. Julia, already precocious, has asked questions about geological time that our guide had brushed aside. I had had no interest in Julia's questions. Instead, I had been fascinated by the idea that cloudy water dripping from a roof could somehow create stone. Four or five drops had splashed on my skin. The water was colder and more penetrating than ordinary water; even its taste was different. And each time a drop fell I was strangely excited, as if I had been touched or even chosen by a process I could not begin to understand, 'Look,' I had said, turning to my sister and showing her a droplet in my palm 'it's a bit of forever.'

Nothing else was said as we climbed the path. Julia was several steps behind me, wheezing slightly. I wondered if her head was already filling with numbers.

My sister had always been intellectually gifted, and years ahead of me even though I was two years older. Numbers and time were Julia's passion as well as her profession; in them she found excitement, meaning, and a sense of order, and for months now she had used their seductive elaborations to prevent herself from brooding. This was a woman who could clearly explain the difference between a sidereal and a tropical year and how Coordinated Universal Time was determined by the oscillations of caesium. Only recently she had published an academic article on Bede's *De Temperum Rationale*, 'On the Reckoning of Time', and I knew that she had become fascinated by the eagle's bone found at Le Placard, 11,000 years old and probably a lunar calendar, and the Earth Mother figurine of Laussel, 27,000 years old, whose incised notches could also be a form of measurement. Some of my colleagues found Julia to be self-absorbed, and my wife had never been able to fully engage with her, but I had grown more and more sympathetic to my sister's focus and honesty. I had always envied her intelligence, and now I envied her courage.

A waiting area had been excavated from the mountain-side. Eight people sat on rough-cut slabs, quietly talking among themselves like witnesses before a hearing. As we arrived, one slapped an insect that had landed on her arm and then wiped the remains from her skin with a tissue.

The entrance to the cave was an artificial arch that had evidently been hacked into the cliff face soon after its discovery. A thick metal door with heavy bolts and padlocks stood open. Inside the first dim chamber a young man could be seen checking handheld lamps that cast shadows upwards on his face. Above the arch was a sign that I managed to read: the cave system was the property of the family who had discovered it a hundred years ago, but all archaeological finds were the property of the University of Madrid. Visitors were limited to a maximum of twelve. Photography was forbidden. The cave opened at ten, with the last admission at five. Even I could calculate the highest possible number of visitors per day,

We sat down and waited. The rest of the group consisted of American academics who were spending their vacation visiting historic sites. One said that she knew that this system wouldn't be anything like as good as Puente Viesgo. Another consulted his watch every two minutes; he'd hoped to be in Toledo by now. Another man, mark-edly overweight, wondered if the cave would be too much of an ordeal. The woman who had killed the insect slapped another. The noise was unexpectedly sharp.

The earlier group came blinking and squinting out of the cave, led by a guide I took to be the patriarch of the family that owned it. He shook hands with each member of his party before they set off down the path, some so unsteadily it seemed they had grown unused to daylight. One even put on a pair of dark glasses before he left, as though he feared the sun.

Stooping so as not to hit our heads our own group filed beneath the arch. Behind it was an excavated chamber with rough walls, an uneven floor, and a counter that had been knocked together from old pieces of wood. Behind it stood our guide, a young man in his mid-twenties, handsome, with a long Andalusian face and eyes that were almost black. As he collected our fees he asked what languages we spoke. In the proximity of the chamber I could detect other people's sweat, perfume, and the snacks they had eaten while waiting. From Julia there came a tired, unwashed smell, although I knew she had taken a long shower that morning.

Some of the group leafed through the half-dozen post-cards that were for sale. They showed rock formations that were suggestive of engineered shapes, outlines of recognis-able animals, an oddly shaped hand stencilled with ochre, and strings of rust-coloured vertical lines like a stylised drawing of broken fences.

Julia picked up a card that showed the lines and angled it so that I could see. As she did, one sleeve slid down her emaciated arm.

'The calendars?' I asked.

She nodded as she peered at the image.

'Anything?'

'I've seen photographs before. Perhaps they're not all shown. I can't judge.'

Lamps were handed out to the visitors, one for each

couple, but the young man kept the largest and brightest for himself. I held the one that Julia and I were to share. The light hollowed her face still further, raising her cheekbones and sharpening her nose. Sometimes when I looked at her I had the uneasy feeling that I was staring into a bewitched mirror that showed my own mortality.

The young man held an open hand to his chest. 'Santiago,' he announced proudly, his eyes shining like black marble. I found myself nodding in response. He said that where we stood had been dug out of the hillside after the discovery, but we would soon be able to see the gap in the earth that his great-grandfather had fallen down when he was a boy looking after the family goats. The cleft had opened into a passageway, and that was where we were going. We were warned to be careful, to stay together, and not to take photographs. And he lifted his lamp to guide us through a fissure through which the overweight man had no trouble squeezing.

After twenty metres in a dark passage we stopped to peer upwards at the original entrance. Through a crooked funnel of rock we could see the sky, and although it seemed to be very far away, as if viewed through the wrong end of a telescope, a draught of clear air swept down on us. It seemed to me that the blue was already darkening.

'This is last daylight you see,' Santiago said, and we set off again.

Conversation, footfall, the noise of breathing and the rustle of clothes were all now eerily distinct, as if noise, like light, was gradually being withdrawn from the world. With each step the cave grew colder. I watched the lamp-light turn the grey bulbous walls into something slimy and organic, and I imagined that we had begun to burrow into the innards of a dead colossus.

In a chamber whose height I could only guess we trod gingerly round stubs of yellowish grey stalagmites. If someone had shouted out, and Julia had timed the echoes, she could have estimated the dimensions of the cavern.

'Tiny drops of water falling for millions of years made these.' Santiago explained, and turned his beam upwards. It faded just as it brushed the tips of a ghostly army of inverted pinnacles. 'We cannot measure how old, just as we cannot measure true length of cave. It is beyond mathematics.'

Her skin made sallow by the glow, Julia smiled and leaned on her pole.

Like stumps of melting pillars that would soon turn to mush, the stalagmites appeared glazed but insubstantial. When I surreptitiously touched one of these it was, or course, utterly solid, but I remained intrigued by the difference between the actuality of the stone and how my vision had interpreted it. I had known the truth, but I had still been misled. In a few seconds of silence we could hear drops of water splashing all around us.

Santiago stood against a massive wall that slanted upwards towards the cavern ceiling. Our group huddled like children as he warned us not to touch the wall behind him. Three metres wide and rising from the floor until it vanished beyond the reach of our lights, it was completely black. The blackness had the matt, absorbent quality of compressed ash.

'Fire,' he said. 'Generation after generation, Old and

New Stone Age people had a fire here. The wall is soot from that fire.'

Someone asked how long it had burned and Santiago shrugged.

'Forty thousand years, maybe more, until the cave is abandoned when the climate grows warmer. We think the fire never went out. It burned all the time. They used it for heat and for cooking food. Families always need shelter.'

I thought of the fire being tended generation upon generation. Nowadays it was scarcely conceivable that sons and daughters should be the same as their parents, or that we should hand on to our children nothing more than a flame. What, I wondered, would Julia hand on to me, and what would I hand on to my wife and whoever came after us: a house, a plot of land, a few photographs, furniture and books, our entries in official registers?

A little farther on and we stopped to peer beneath a rock shelf while Santiago shone his light on a slightly concave wall. Outlined in black were images of bison, deer, and ibex.

'Neolithic,' he said; 'Maybe eight thousand years before Christ. We found tools here that were tested by the University of Madrid, I have my degree there. Accelerator mass spectroscopy calculates the years. Here the pigment is charcoal and animal fat. Neolithic people use charcoal for paint, but Palaeolithic people use ochre. Some experts say the animals are dead. They are here on the wall like animals that have been killed. So maybe this is a kind of magic, a wish, a prayer.'

We studied the outlines. Lanterns held in unsteady hands gave an illusory sense of movement to the images, as if the animals were rising out of their stone background.

Now there was an upward slope into which irregular modern steps had been cut and a rudimentary handrail fitted. A silent flurry of bats peeled from the ceiling and settled again.

'Bats used to drink here,' Santiago indicated as we entered the next chamber. A broad pool took our lights. Beneath its surface a few dozen coins glinted on the reddish floor. As soon as I saw them I remembered my nightmare. For a few moments, until I regained my composure, I felt dizzy.

'Metal poisons the water so the bats cannot drink,' Santiago said gloomily. 'Do not throw coins.' Someone asked how many bats lived in the caves. 'The largest colonies live in parts we cannot visit. There will be thousands.'

Julia murmured in my ear. 'You could estimate them from the number leaving at night to feed,' she said.

And, then, suddenly, life seemed to leave her face. She shuddered and raised her free hand to her forehead but did not touch it. I moved closer and put my arm around her shoulders. She seemed to be little more than bone.

'I'm all right,' she whispered. 'You can let go.'

I kept my arm where it was.

'We can go back,' I murmured.

Santiago had noticed our discomfort. 'If anyone cannot go on,' he announced, 'we can leave them here with their lanterns and collect them on the return. But they must stay here and not move.'

'I'm fine,' Julia said. I took my arm away reluctantly.

Santiago stared at us for a moment and then motioned us so that we stood a few paces away from the rest of the group. He raised his light so that it was close as an interrogator's to Julia's face.

'I want to see the calendars,' she told him, and took a deep breath of the chill air. 'That's why I'm here. I'm a specialist. I want to understand them.'

'University professors cannot understand them,' he answered.

'I *am* a university professor.'

Santiago considered for a moment before speaking again.

'You are very sick. I see it in your eyes. I saw it when you entered the cave.'

'I can go on.'

'We are walking for three kilometres inside our mountain. There are many steps, climbs, places to fall. It is not easy for a sick person.'

'I need to see those calendars.'

'I'll help my sister if she needs me,' I said. As a comparison I nodded towards the back of the overweight man whose wheezing was still audible.

Santiago made up his mind.

'Come then,' he said, and strode forward to take the lead again. I touched Julia's elbow and we shuffled to the end of a line of swaying lanterns.

Now we passed through a gallery of columns that were fused stalactites and stalagmites, and for a hundred metres or more it seemed that rock the colour of old ivory had been carved into musculature, tendons and cellular traceries like those of a lung. Light smeared the vitrified surfaces and brought out faint traces of red among gradations of yellow and grey. When everyone fell silent we could hear splashing noises, but it seemed that the water had become viscous and that somehow its fall had slowed.

Even more keenly now I had the sense that we were being led through the remains of a creature so vast that no one had been able to recognise that we were moving through its vertebrae and ligaments.

At several points Santiago indicated a particular bizarre or geometrical formation. One was said to resemble the face of a Renaissance Christ. He angled his light to bring out the contours of the face.

I murmured in Julia's ear. 'Do you see it?'

'Of course I see it. That doesn't mean that it's actually there.'

'No?'

'The brain makes sense of meaningless images. That's how its sensory and intellectual systems got our ancestors out of places like this.'

Now we headed into the very heart of the mountain. The way was always upward, the passages even more hazardous. Bats unglued themselves from the ceiling, moved stickily across it, and then folded their wings and settled again. At the side of the path were holes blacker than carbon, the entrances to caverns that plunged for five or ten metres, maybe more. United by feelings of privilege and danger, group members began to talk freely about their lives. Their voices lacked conviction, as if the cave system had removed their honesty. Neither Julia nor I said anything.

Santiago halted at a rock layered like the shell of a gigantic mollusc. His breath misted in the lantern's pall.

It seemed that the air we breathed had lain within the caves for millennia.

'Beyond here are sinkholes, large shafts hollowed out of the rock. Soon there is a very, very deep one. Please; everyone be extra careful. I have warned you.'

We edged our way through yet another narrow passage. I could not understand why a Palaeolithic tribe should have felt compelled to explore the farthest reaches of such a complex and hazardous system. They would have had no light other than pieces of wood or rush dipped in tallow, and every step would have been hazardous. An extinguished flame would have marooned them in blackness so absolute that a move of just a few metres could have been fatal. And now I began to wonder if my sister's resolve to reach the calendars was more than just a desire for rational and explicable insight. Perhaps Julia had speculated that these passages and burrows, and the markings they contained, would somehow clarify the purpose of her own life.

Santiago halted and lowered his lantern to illuminate several dry shallow pits, no more than a few centimes deep. Within them were pieces of reddish gravel, some of it granules, some little more than grit.

'Ochre,' he announced, and the lifted his arm so that light swept across the nearest wall.

The rock face was covered with short red vertical lines the colour of dried blood. There were perhaps two hundred in total, painted next to each other in about twenty groups, with no group sharing the same number of lines.

'Forty thousand years before Christ,' Santiago said. 'Not charcoal but red ochre and animal fat. People marked the wall like this.'

He drew an extended index finger through the air. I looked at Julia, who was staring fixedly at the lines, her eyes as reflective as glass. The light erased colour from her face and gave her skin a waxen sheen.

'Very strange,' Santiago said. 'Calendar was painted on wall next to sinkhole. Shaft is hundred metres deep, maybe more.'

He swung his lamp again to reveal that he was guarding a circular black hole in the floor behind him. Light touched its upper lip but penetrated no further.

Julia stepped close to the wall and leaned forward on her stick. I held the light so that she could study the markings more easily. After a short while she moved farther along the wall to concentrate on the next set. Santiago watched carefully, his own light directed at the ground. The rest of the group stood in silence, like mute witnesses

She turned to me, her thin wasted face showing no sign of comprehension.

Santiago spoke quietly. 'They are impossible to understand,' he said.

'It's not a calendar,' Julia said.

He did not answer. The group waited. Julia went on. The closeness of the walls took the pith from her voice and left it a husk.

'They can't be calendars. They have nothing to do with the phases of the sun or moon. There are no ratios or sequences, no lunar intervals, no solstices, no equinoxes. I don't know what they are.'

Santiago's voice was consoling. 'No one knows,' he agreed.

'I can't make any sense of them,' Julia said hopelessly.

She looked at me as if she had failed me personally, as well as herself, as well as posterity. 'I can't solve them but there must be a solution. There was a purpose but we can't know what it was.'

'Maybe to do with this,' Santiago said.

He turned his light on a part of the cave wall that had been kept in shadow until that moment. It showed the image of a human hand, stencilled with ochre. The hand appeared curiously misshapen, with the thumb noticeably longer than the fingers.

Santiago held his own hand next to it, palm outwards. The chill of the cave closed around me.

'This is how it was done,' he explained. 'The back of the hand is placed on the stone and paint blown across it. This explains long thumb and short fingers. Person's hand is held steady by others. Tribes still do this in other parts of the world. They do it when person is dead.'

For several seconds no one spoke. The shadows on the walls seemed not to move. On all sides the cave system branched into blackness and branched again, into chambers and veins and capillaries, limitless, eternal, and immeasurable.

Julia raised her free hand towards the lines of markings. 'Maybe they're a tally,' she said.

Santiago's eyes were deepest black.

'That's the only explanation,' she insisted. 'They were counting something.'

I threw light on the marks again.

'Tally,' Santiago repeated.

'A numbered account,' Julia explained; 'a record, a register, a score, a reckoning.'

'A reckoning,' Santiago repeated, relishing the word. 'Like this,' he went on, and raised his hand to count us all. He numbered Julia first, and then the overweight man, and then the rest of the group, and lastly me. I felt that ice had closed around my heart.

'That's right,' Julia agreed, her voice little more than a whisper, 'a reckoning.'

We looked at each other, brother and sister, people who had led shared lives, people who knew that one was ending.

Julia held out her free hand to me. It was trembling with cold and her fingers were closed.

'Look,' she said.

I raised the lantern to see more clearly.

A droplet of cloudy water shivered in the centre of her palm.

Salt Lagoons

Wゴゴ HILE I AM driving between the salt hills I suddenly
remember being told that they mark the northernmost limit of wild flamingoes. I cannot remember who
said this, but I am somehow certain that it must be true.

I stop the car and look round. The reclamation zone
is empty beneath the brine-stifled air, its artificial lagoons
wine-red or jade with bacterial growth, its locked sluice
gates sparking with crusted salt. I watch for several minutes,
but nothing moves except for air rising in waves from the
evaporation pans. After a while I drive away disappointed.
I have never seen flamingoes in the wild, but often they
move silently through my dreams.

There is one last shrinking pond, one more retaining
dyke and then I see the town outlined against a hazy glittering arc of sea. High stone battlements rise above a straggle of twentieth-century houses. For years I have studied
plans and photographs of these fortifications; I have even
complied statistics of the Crusader vessels that sailed from
quays that have long since been lost beneath delta silt and
invasive grass.

The mind is a sly creature. The Taj Mahal and the

Eiffel Tower are familiar to millions who have never been to India or France. Everyone recognises places that have never visited. So it is with me and this town.

But it is chance and not destiny that leads me south. The conference has ended on time but there is a day to spare before my return flight. My paper was well received, and afterwards a fellow professor of medieval history asked how long it was since I had visited the old port, as he could assure me that its fortifications were still extremely well preserved.

Of course I knew that, but dared not confess that I had never visited the town. When I was a younger man I had intended to stay for a few days, but at first I had lingered elsewhere, and then there had been a cross-channel ferry to catch. So I had never been to the place that had become a tiny part of my academic life.

'It's a few years since my last visit,' I lied.

'But my dear North,' my colleague said with cloying familiarity, 'you must go back, and soon.' Then, checking my name to the identity tag safety-pinned to my lapel, he became even more familiar to press his point. 'Laurence, your paper was fascinating and thorough if a little too statistical. A sprinkling of testimony from, say, Fulcher or Albert of Aachen would have given it some depth and an impression of life as it was once lived.'

It was, of course, a rebuke, but rather than stoke an academic rivalry I merely smiled thinly and turned away. I am sensitive to criticism and sometimes think that my work may be slightly remote, too reliant on abstraction, graphs, and tables. And surely my town must be one of those places in the world that still retain an unmistakable imprint of the past. This is the reason why I have driven south, and this is the reason why I am parking beneath these walls.

I walk under a stone archway across cobblestones as shiny as fused glass. Beyond is a sunlit area that must once have been a medieval courtyard but which is now a town square with cafés, parasols, souvenir shops, and a hotel. Festival pennants hang motionless from lines strung between the buildings. At the centre of the square there is a fountain with a metal drinking spout. As I watch, young couples put their mouths to the glittering stream and surface laughing. Water runs down their chins and arms and spots their thin summer clothes.

All the café tables are full, but just up the hotel steps there is a small balcony which is deserted except for a woman in sunglasses. She sits there on her own, apparently studying the people in the square just below her.

I walk up the steps. There are only four tables, so I sit at the one farthest away from the woman and order a drink. She is wearing a pale blue dress with buttons up the front, a loosely tied chiffon scarf, and her legs are crossed. Her dark insolent lenses study me while the waiter takes my order. For a few seconds I imagine her being charmed by whatever I say, but for the moment I cannot imagine what that would be.

When the waiter returns with my drink the woman summons him with a confidently raised hand. They speak rapidly to each other. He nods and returns to the gloomy interior of the hotel.

'You need not pay for that,' she tells me in lightly accented English.

I am startled by her presumption but also intrigued that she has recognised my nationality. I wonder if the waiter has told her. When I look into the hotel I can see that he is watching me from the shade of the doorway. As soon as our eyes meet he drops his gaze and turns away.

I begin to insist that I'll pay for my own drink, but the woman interrupts.

'I did not think you would sit so far away.'

It had not occurred to me to sit near to her, and I begin to wonder about her motivations.

'There is no one here,' she tells me, indicating the next chair.

I am not sure how to react. 'I don't want to intrude,' I say.

Her silence is like an investigator's, intended to foster guilt.

I clear my throat and continue. 'Besides, you look as if you're waiting for someone.'

'But I am,' she answers. 'I have been here on this day for twenty years.'

'It's a special day?'

A moments silence hangs in the air and is filled by the noise from the square. Eventually she answers.

'The Feast of the Assumption.'

'I see. You speak English very well.'

She stands up, the chair legs squeal on the tiles, and she walks to my table and sits opposite me. I can smell her perfume.

'I teach it. Surely that's no surprise?'

'No,' I answer, perplexed.

She takes off her glasses and gazes at me. Her face

is pale and intense, her eyes wide. She does not blink but continues to stare. Instinctively I lean further away. Sunlight crawls across the space between us.

'You have a mark across your forehead,' she says. 'Was it an accident?'

The observation is so unexpected that I raise my fingers to the scar before dropping them again.

'I was a passenger in the front seat of a car. It happened years ago. I remember everything up until just before the impact.'

'Everything? You're sure?'

'Of course.'

I am annoyed by this stranger's impertinence and uncertain why she should have chosen to talk to me at all.

She lifts a hand to indicate the medieval walls. A gold wedding ring shines on one finger.

'You must have come to walk the ramparts. Is that right?'

'I have an interest, yes.'

'Everyone who visits here wants to walk the ramparts. Even people with no sense of history want to do that. But I'm sure you know all about this town. We could walk the ramparts together. You could lecture me.'

I have never been propositioned like this. Unwittingly, I grin from sudden embarrassment. This woman must expect me to recognise her needs in the same way that I recognise the town, but they are shadowy and uncertain.

I want to stand up and leave but my curiosity and excitement are aroused. And a part of me feels vulnerable, as though she is touching an emotion I have long since forgotten.

'From the battlements you can see our beach,' she goes on.

'Right,' I say. I'd studied the map and knew the flattened contours of town, river and coast.

'You think I mean the town beach?'

'Don't you?'

She waits for a few seconds before she answers. 'No, I mean *our* beach; the one next to the sea. Yours and mine.'

I do not know how to answer, other than to say that I have no intention of visiting a beach with her, but I keep silent.

'It is twenty years since we shared that beach,' she says. 'I always knew you would come back.'

Suddenly the heat and light intensify. When I try to meet her eyes they are so forceful that I have to look away.

I do not know who this stranger is, and I am suddenly scared that I have been selected, picked out by a woman who is disturbed and possibly dangerous. I draw back further and am ready to leave, but she reaches across the table and closes her hand tightly around mine.

'You don't remember me, do you?'

'I'm sorry,' I say, and attempt to lean further away. She does not relax her grip.

'Your memories cannot have been completely destroyed. If they had been, you would not have come back.'

'I've never been here before. Never. I have an interest in the Middle Ages and that's the reason I decided to visit. I'm not here for anything else.'

At last she lets go of my hand. I decide to thank her for the drink but to leave it unfinished and get away with as much dignity as I can.

'I know why you are lying,' she announces with sudden determination. 'You are jealous and hurt because of this.'

She lifts the hand with the wedding ring and then continues.

'You cannot be surprised. What did you expect me to do? I heard nothing from you, ever. Did you not marry?'

'Yes,' I tell her.

'And where is your wife today?'

'She's dead. She's been dead a long time.'

'In a car? The same accident that marked you?'

I nod.

'And did you love her?'

'Of course I did.'

She nods thoughtfully. 'I have two girls. They are in their teens now. And you?'

'No. We hadn't been married long. Look, I'm sorry, but this is absurd. I don't know what to say other than that your memory is at fault. You've got the wrong man.'

'No, I have the right man: the only one.'

I shake my head firmly.

'I know you better than you know yourself,' the woman insists.

'I don't think so.'

'I *know* you. Your name is Laurence North. You teach history: medieval history. You were always interested in the Crusades.'

Everything becomes insubstantial for a few moments, and then I remember that my identity badge from the conference is still pinned to my shirt.

'When you first visited our town you told me you were

studying for a degree,' she continues. 'Today you have come back,'

Still numbed, I nod automatically. She leans close and continues.

'You told me you would give up your studies.'

'No. I would never say that.'

'When we became lovers you promised me. You swore that all you wanted was to be with me. We talked of living together in a tiny house beside the bay. You said that all we needed was each other. And now you do not even call me by my name.'

I struggle to think of a reply but before I can speak the woman reaches out and touches my lips with her fingertips. The contact is strange, thrilling, arousing.

'I can never forget,' she murmurs. 'I have been watching you from the moment you walked through that archway. I knew it was you. My heart raced like the heart of a young girl. I recognised your face, your body, the way you walked, the way you looked round. When you speak it is with the voice that speaks in my memory. If I were blind and deaf I would still recognise the touch of your hand on my skin.'

I look at the high battlements, sharp with sunlight. There are no shadows. The woman moves even closer, I can feel the warmth of her breath.

'What are you thinking now, Laurence? That when a crash took your wife from you it robbed you of your past as well? Listen to me; a part of your memory has been stolen, but it has not gone forever. Something you cannot quite understand has made you come back to this place on this day. The past buoys us all up, like salt in the sea.'

I think of the evaporation ponds, the sluice gate, and

the high crystalline mounds of salt that lined the approach road.

Her gaze does not leave my face.

'I won't tell you my name. Soon you will remember it. You will begin to remember everything. How we rode white horses along the strand. How we came round the horn of the bay and saw that in front of us there were hundreds of flamingoes feeding in the shallow waters.'

My hand jerks a little. She clutches it tightly.

'You told me you had never seen flamingoes in the wild, and I told you that they cannot live farther north.'

I shake my head. She goes on.

'We discovered lonely dunes where we lay naked in hollows filled with heat and brightness and the smell of our bodies after making love. Soon you will be able to remember all this, Laurence. You will remember how, on his day many years ago when we were young, we drank from the fountain in the square and swore that we would never forget our love. And then we promised each other that we would meet here again on the Day of the Assumption, even if it was a year, two years, even five before we could. I have waited for you for four times five years, and now at last you have come back to me.'

My sense of self wavers in her gaze. 'I can't—' I begin, but she interrupts.

'What other kind of proof do you need?'

I can say nothing.

Her voice is tolerant but determined. 'It will take only a little time. There is a room for you here at this hotel. It has been booked for this festival night for nineteen years. Tonight you must sleep alone: I have a husband who cannot know about you. Tomorrow we will meet on the battlements. And then we must decide what to do, and how best to share our future. And if you want more proof, tomorrow I will bring you photographs that only I have ever seen. I keep them hidden at my home.'

'Photographs of us?'

'Tomorrow,' she says.

And then she stands up and touches my scar, moving her fingers along it like someone consoling an injured child.

'They were taken at out beach. Tonight, at nine, I will go back there to watch the festival across the water. I will be on my own. Come with me. It has been too long a wait.'

'Yes,' I promise, 'I'll be there.'

But I can remember nothing of the past that she has conjured so artfully, and I tell myself that this is the most efficient way to be rid of her.

Before she leaves the woman puts a hand on the back of my neck and kisses me briefly on the forehead. All the time she looks into my eyes as if searching for my lost memory.

As I watch her walk down the steps and cross the square, without even turning to look at me, I know that my curiosity and excitement will lead me to the shore this evening.

In the hotel I ask about the room. The receptionist is conspiratorial and I sense that he and the waiter, and possibly others, have been spying on me.

'We have expected you for many years,' he says quietly. It is as if he has at last come face to face with someone whose existence he had often doubted.

'Did the lady book the room in her name or mine?' I ask.

'Always in her own,' he answers.

I have no need to ask the next question. Eager to demonstrate understanding and fellowship in matters of the heart, he turns his booking screen towards me and indicates a name with his finger. I do not recognise it.

'Your Isabelle has a new last name,' he murmurs. 'I am told that her husband is a trusting man. I can, if you wish, amend the booking to your name. But if I do that, I will need your passport.'

I shake my head. 'Best leave things as they are.'

'As you wish, Mr North,' he says.

And once again I wish that I had removed my conference identity badge.

Some hours later I am waiting on the road beside the dark beach. Before long a small car drives up and is parked under a dim street light. The woman steps from it. I walk up to her as she presses the key to lock the door. Moths career through the air above our heads.

'Isabelle,' I say.

Tears come to her eyes. They brighten in the street light's yellowish pall.

'I knew you would remember,' she says, and smooths my forehead as though the scar could be erased by the motions of her hand. 'You are still him, still my Laurence. Even without a complete memory, you are still the man I have been waiting for.'

'That's right,' I tell her.

Without further words she leads me down a short flight of wooden steps onto a beach the colour of mummy-cloth.

Everything is calm. There are waterfront lights a

kilometre away across the curve of the bay. The ragged noises of singing and car horns carry easily across the black water.

Along the edge of the sea there is a line of shallow dunes. Their depressions are filled with dark figures so close to each other that they cannot be told apart. Isabelle finds a deserted hollow and we sit together. The sand is bone-dry, still warm from the sun, and our bodies are touching.

I know that whoever shared this beach with her all those years ago, it was not me.

Red and green fireworks explode along the far corniche and the water reflects them. Isabelle puts her hand on my chest and leans her head on my shoulder.

I watch rockets climb up high, their inverted trails bending and spangling in the water's low, broad ripples. When they burn out seconds later I can hear the hiss as the hot casings tumble into the black sea.

Back at the hotel I cannot sleep at all. At first I am exhilarated, but then guilty.

My room overlooks the square. The fountain water has been turned off, and I think that if it was still falling I would leave my room and put my mouth to the spout just to taste its icy, salt-free purity.

Not until dawn do I become frightened. I do not want to meet Isabelle again and I do not want to see her photographs: I might recognise the man within them.

I leave before breakfast and drive away just as the dawn begins to break.

Somewhere in the middle of the reclamation works my

decisiveness falters and I stop the car beside a high bank. Around me shadows retract as the sun rises, and one gives a spindly, flickering movement. I turn to look at the top of the bank. Its rim is edged with sunlight, and from it a flamingo stares down at me with fathomless unblinking eyes.

For a moment I do not move, but then I get out of the car. The bird flaps disdainfully out of sight.

I leave the car and struggle up the steep rake of the bank. Brine reels in the senses as the dawn heightens around me. When I stand on the summit I look own onto an evaporation pool of greenish water ringed by contours of salt.

Hundreds of flamingoes have settled in the pond. I watch them pick their elegant, mysterious way through the scummy water, their colour heightening as the sun rises higher. They are all silent. Not one makes a sound.

I watch the birds for several minutes before I return to the car and drive away. As I pass the northernmost salt hill I notice that a mechanical grab has begun to gouge it apart so that a deep fissure scars its brow. And then I watch the hill become smaller in my mirror as the distance grows between us.

In the town that I have deserted the sun is climbing higher over ramparts that at this hour of the morning will still be empty.

The Face of the Earth

THE CITY LIES at the continent's very edge. The young woman had spent her first few days there, acclimatising herself in a tall concrete-and-glass hotel overlooking the corniche with its beach clubs, sunbathers, and hawkers of cheap trinkets. Three years later I took a room in the same hotel and waited for a London flight to bring her father to me.

I paid two boys to guard the Land Rover. They took turns to squat beside it while their cousins scavenged the rubbish hoppers at the back of the building. On the day before Pryce's arrival I drove into town to make the final arrangements for our journey, and that evening I sat on my own in the hotel garden. An artificial waterfall had been built there, with a circular basin crowded by foliage and floodlights whose glass panels were black with mosquitoes.

Pryce had forwarded me a copy of his latest book. It was dedicated to his daughter's memory. The book was a risible but faintly touching confection of incorrect archaeology, wishful thinking, and geomancy. Photocopies of reviews from occult journals had been slipped inside the volume as if these somehow proved its worth.

I leafed through it again, but was still unable to read more than a few pages. Eventually I gave up trying and slipped it into my shoulder bag. I was tense enough to need a smoke of kif. It was a relaxation and a vice that I sometimes allowed myself.

Doormen kept the hotel entrance clear, but within less than twenty metres their influence waned. Berber women sat on the ground trying to sell prickly pears that had already begin to rot with the heat. Hustlers, beggars and unofficial guides crowded round any visitor; they even tried to talk to me as I hailed a taxi. They wished to be my guide, they needed alms, and they could get me good fun, young girls, young boys, whatever Sir wanted. I brushed them all aside. I had years of experience behind me.

The café was at the city's edge, where squat buildings gave way to a straggle of shacks. The night air was heavy and treacherous with the smell of kif. I watched while the leaves were diced on a wooden board and mixed with tobacco and then I bought several pipe's worth. I smoked it while I drank hot mint tea and sat at a table beneath a rope of coloured lights while local music droned in the background. It was not long before my body became pleasantly torpid and my mind alert. The world rose in front of me like a display.

When I left the café I was both refreshed and bitter. On the road back I watched from the taxi as one of the beggars was led home from the city centre. I had often noticed him; he was difficult to ignore. He was unusually tall, well over six feet, with a labourer's frame but sightless eyes as dead as marble. From just after dawn to well after dusk, led by a young girl who must have been his daughter, he walked the streets with a begging-bowl held out before him. Now they were returning to whatever it was that they called home. Soon they would sleep and then, in a few hours' time, they would begin their circuit again.

I had realised that Pryce's dust jacket portrait was too youthful, but I was still surprised at his deterioration when I met him the next day. It was less than three years since the official inquiry, and in that time he had become a much older man. Tinted glasses with round lenses and metal frames made him look both sinister and feeble, and he often placed a hand on his scalp, fingers spread, as if expressing forgetfulness.

On the way from the airport he did nothing but talk about our planned journey and how long it would take, and within half an hour of his arrival he insisted that I spread a map across a table in the empty lobby. Pryce bent over it like a character from Rider Haggard peering at the blanks of *terra incognita*. When he took off his glasses to study our route I noticed that the hooks had left indentations in the flesh behind his ears. He turned to me: his nose was thin and his blue eyes were like ice beneath water.

'You needn't worry,' he said, as though he could read my thoughts, 'I've made more severe journeys than this.'

I nodded. 'Maybe when you were younger and had more stamina – and hadn't lost a daughter.'

'I've hired you as the ideal guide,' he said, pointing at the end of my pencilled line on the map. 'My health will last as far as our destination.'

Alongside the map he placed something that was wrapped in a square of red satin, and then he unfolded it as carefully as if he were bringing to light a treasure of great value.

'This is her diary,' he explained. 'We must follow it without deviation. I need to be as close to Lucy as I possibly can. That means that it's essential that we start tomorrow. Even the days of the week must be the same.'

Pryce was reluctant to let me handle the diary, seeming to forget that I was the one who had taken it from his daughter's hired Toyota and brought it back with me.

I had known it must be there, and had searched in a kind of fever. Eventually I found it deep in a side pocket along with her mobile phone. Of course I read the last entry first; as perhaps it would reveal the secret of her disappearance. But there was nothing, for the last entry was dated two days ago. I remember trembling with relief. Lucy had been a travel writer and had chronicled the journey as obsessively as a cartographer, but there was no illumination for anyone who wanted to follow her beyond the point where she had written *I'll reach the frescoes tomorrow.*

'Graham,' I said, 'I understand why you want to do this, but I must tell you that you won't find any trace of your daughter.'

He nodded absent-mindedly, as though listening to advice he did not wish to hear.

I pressed on. 'Things will still be the same as they were when I came across her vehicle. If I'd arrived a day or two earlier then perhaps they'd have been different. But I can't help that. I wouldn't even have visited the outcrops if I hadn't been considering taking a group of archaeologists to them.'

'I understand. I've thought about it a lot, so of course I understand,'

'Listen, Graham: your daughter has vanished forever, and we'll never know why or how. There's nothing to hope for, so please don't do that. It would be pointless. There is no solution.'

'There must be. And it can't be the obvious one.'

I sighed. 'When the police introduced us I felt sorry for you. Everyone did but no one could help. I agreed to take you on this journey so you can come to terms with her death, but a part of me knows that it's unwise.'

'Dead?' he asked. 'You're still convinced that my daughter is dead?'

'You must have accepted that by now.'

He shook his head. 'Not in the sense that you mean, no. And I had to persuade you to take me because for a long time you didn't want to. You thought that photographs of the site would be enough.'

'I'm still not convinced that I did right to agree. I don't think this will solve anything. You're not going to come away feeling more settled. It will probably make you worse.'

Later, when he asked, I took Pryce to the hotel's upper story. At first he paced he length of the viewing platform as if measuring it, but then he quietened down and gazed out over the sea,

'She did this before she started,' he said. 'She says in her diary that Europe was a distant hazy smudge beyond the freighters passing through the straits.'

'You can see it today,' I told him casually.

'I'm not blind yet,' he snapped.

I said nothing else. Europe was invisible.

◊

For days we followed Lucy's trail through small, isolated towns where tethered goats fed on little else but thorn. I knew these places well, but Pryce had never travelled such roads. I watched him warily as each day sapped his strength and he lay exhausted and sweating beneath one of my mosquito nets in the bedrooms of tiny hotels.

He created his own journal of our travels, each day whispering it into a small recording device that he packed away carefully when he had finished. I wondered if he was scared that I might steal it and listen to what he had said, so after a few days I told him that I had no interest in eavesdropping. Pryce smiled at me warmly but still packed away his device as if it were the next most important thing to his daughter's diary.

At each cluster of buildings he produced photographs of Lucy and asked if anyone knew his daughter, or if she had been seen within the last three years. Like a searcher in an Edwardian adventure story, he even asked if there were rumours of a tall blonde woman living among a group of nomads. Some reported that they could indeed remember such a woman passing through the villages: This was no surprise, as Lucy would have been a strikingly unusual figure in such surroundings. Besides, the police had been this way before us, showing the same photograph, asking the same questions, and villagers such as these always have the clearest of memories

Before the final stage of our journey, as I was loading the vehicle with jerricans of diesel filled at the last pump before the desert, I tried to persuade Pryce that we had gone far enough.

'You know whatever there is to know,' I told him. 'We won't find out anything else.'

'I'm sure that can't be true.'

'There's nothing now but miles of rock and sand. You've seen the police photos of your daughter's car; it looks exactly as I found it. As for the outcrops and the frescoes, you already know what they look like. There's nothing to discover.'

He answered calmly.

'Of course I know what they look like. It's the atmosphere I have to experience. Photographs and written reports only give a hint of what is real.'

'Graham, let's go back. Now. It would be the sensible course of action. I don't like to see you jeopardise your health in this way.'

'You think I should worry about my health at a time like this? When we've come so far? I paid you to take me to that place and that's where we'll go.'

I stood closer. Sweat glazed his skin and soaked his shirt with dark patches.

'Forget about my fee,' I said 'You can have the money back, all of it, just so long as you see sense.'

'But I do see sense. That's why we mustn't stop now.' In an act that seemed oddly helpless, he pushed back his hat and spread his fingers across his head.

I slammed the last jerrican into place, as if the noise gave value to my plea.

'Whatever you say,' I said.

While I monitored our route and constantly checked out position, Pryce seemed mainly concerned with Lucy's diary. For him its notations and rough sketches were a more valid guide than my scrupulous GPS measurements and calculations. A bed of glassy lava, snapped into shards, was just as she had described it. The desiccated corpse of a camel, its hide tanned by the sun, was still uncomfortably near to an oasis once used by the salt caravans. During the day the heat was so intense that mirages shivered at the horizon. At night the temperature plummeted, and we could look up into a chilling clarity of stars.

It took two days across barren desert before we reached our destination. We had been scanning ahead as eagerly as sailors searching for land, but of course I was the first to see the outcrops.

'We're almost there,' I said as calmly as I could, and glanced at Pryce. His face was set with determination but the expression in his eyes was hidden behind his glasses. 'Remember that things appear to be closer than they actually are,' I added.

And I thought of how the investigating officer, an over-weight policeman with a thin moustache, had been eager to take me into his confidence. Perhaps this was because he had not actually visited the site, but instead relied on reports from his lieutenants.

None of Lucy Pryce's clothes had been stolen, he had told me. Her rented Toyota had been left untouched, but the memory card had been taken from her Nikon. Also her mobile phone and laptop were missing after apparently being switched off two days before I came on the scene.

I had waited for the officer to say more. He moved

something across his desk, moved it back, and then lowered his voice.

All the signs, he murmured, of a rape by a group of ignorant nomads who had panicked and then murdered the girl.

I said I thought it improbable that nomads would act in such a manner, but speculation carried him away on a surge. Perhaps, he said, before desire overtook them, they had become friendly with Lucy. Perhaps she had even photographed them standing against the frescoes. They would have given local colour to the shots, and scale to the paintings. Afterwards they had had enough cunning to destroy the evidence. As for the woman, well, perhaps they had slit her throat and buried her out in the desert. Or perhaps they had simply left her alone. Confused, distressed, and probably severely beaten, she could have wandered off and died anywhere.

It made sense to agree that he might be right.

If only I had not searched the vehicle when I found it, the officer added sadly; then perhaps the police would have had a few more fingerprints to work on.

Before I could protest, he agreed that I had done the right thing. If he had discovered an abandoned vehicle he, too, would have acted in the same way. I smiled inwardly at the thought of him making such a demanding journey.

The outcrops rose out of the land in a cluster of smooth humps and turrets, the tallest pointing upwards, an obelisk ground smooth by scorching winds. A few palms had rooted into the cracks like forlorn signals for water.

I parked the Land Rover in front of the pointing finger. We were at the exact spot where Lucy had parked her own vehicle.

Pryce climbed out and stood in sun that was as brilliant as a searchlight. In front of him the red column reached up to heaven. He did not say anything. I wondered if, for him, the air was filled with invisible silent forces.

'We can spend one night here,' I told him gruffly, 'and then we have to leave.'

'She must have been here for at least two days."

'Look,' I answered, 'it doesn't matter how long she was here. We only know the dates when the diary stops and the phone was cut off, and the date when I arrived to find a deserted vehicle which turned out to have been hired by her. Let's say she walked away about two days before that.'

Pryce took a few steps away and put his hands on a smooth face of rock, instantly withdrawing them because it was hot to the touch. When he turned back to me he looked both foolish and helpless, like a man being gradually deserted by reality.

'We must stay longer,' he pleaded.

'Graham, I'm responsible for your safety. You've already pushed yourself too far. I wouldn't like you to die of a stroke or dehydration or have some sort of seizure. At least I'm here to help. I don't care how experienced she was, Lucy should have had someone with her.'

'You really think that's what happened to her, don't you? But she wouldn't just wander off. And there was nothing wrong with the Toyota.'

'That's the better explanation. The other one is that a

group of bandits found her. You wouldn't want to think too much about that.'

'Do you think I haven't?'

'She was a woman on her own.' I said patiently. 'She must have ignored all the advice she was given. Anything could have happened to her: anything. At one point the police even suspected that I had something to do with it.'

He gave a brief, dismissive snort. 'The police always look for the most obvious explanation. I'm sorry you were under suspicion.'

I shook my head. 'I can't blame the police. But at least they have theories. You have none.'

'Haven't you read my book?'

I said nothing. He wagged his finger at me as school-masters must have done to him in his youth.

'If you'd read it, if you'd *thought* about what I wrote, you would realise that what we see all around us is just the surface world. There are other worlds folded into this one but hidden from us. Gifted people are given a chance to see those worlds. A few are even allowed to enter them and remain there. History is full of unexplained disappearances.'

'I don't believe in earth magic.'

Pryce inclined his head and looked at me over the rims of his glasses, as if to indicate that he would listen to my protests no matter how ridiculous he found them. His tolerance angered me, and I went on.

'I don't believe in parallel universes or reincarnation or that past events are somehow still here and detectable. Just as I don't believe that there are Tibetan monks who are six hundred years old or that rocks in Death Valley move across its floor of their own accord. Should I tell you what else it would be sensible not to believe in?'

'I'm sure you could go on for a long time. But I'll tell you what I believe. I believe that somehow Lucy's spirit is still here, even though we can't see or hear her.'

I shook my head. 'That's impossible. If she's still here then she's certainly dead, maybe buried out in the sand where we would never find her. I understand why you don't want to accept that, but it would help if you faced the truth. Forget about your mad theories. You're not here to write another of your crazy books. Try to face reality.'

'Reality?' he asked, and appeared genuinely puzzled. 'But you're the one who refuses to face reality.'

I shrugged, exasperated. 'I'm not getting through to you, am I?'

Pryce ignored he question. 'And we must stay here for at least three days, I paid for that.'

'We'll see,' I said. But I wanted to leave here as quickly as possible.

Within the outcrops there are fissures, gullies, pathways; beneath them are crevices and caves; and at the centre is an area that Pryce insisted on calling a cathedral. This is an open space, about thirty yards wide, in an east-facing gulley whose sandstone walls curve above the head as if forming an unfinished dome. To me it is an entirely natural formation, if somewhat freakish. I avoid it if I can - it makes me feel edgy and oversensitive. For Pryce, however, the cathedral was enigmatic, mystical, and almost holy.

Now that we had finally reached our destination his energy had returned, and he was eager to explore the outcrops and study the frescoes. Sometimes he pushed his glasses onto his forehead and scrutinised the pigments like a jeweller examining precious stones. Often he insisted we walk across inclined slabs or scramble beneath overhangs just to reach the less accessible paintings.

There are hundreds, perhaps thousands, of images. They have been painted in a deeper red than the rock, but sometimes there is a splash of white or yellow. They portray an idealised world of people living among a richness of water, vegetation, and animals. Sometimes Pryce commented on them for my benefit. Here are hippopotamus and leopard, he would say, animals that vanished from the region thousands of years ago; here are sheep and cattle, showing the extent of animal domestication; and here are horses drawing chariots, proving that this was a developed, mobile culture which could have escaped from the encroaching desert if it had wanted to.

Most of all Pryce stared at the human figures, and often seemed as absorbed in them as a visitor gazing at a masterpiece in a gallery. Some are nothing more than stick figures, but others are the size of giants. They are always in a group and never drawn singly. They have featureless faces the colour of faded blood, but about their bodies are finely detailed necklaces, shields, cloaks, spears. Some wear animal horns, others wear plumes, helmets, and crowns of what appear to be long blades of grass.

'Look,' Pryce explained, 'these are hunters, and these are farmers using a system of irrigation for their crops. This is a group of women selling fruit – here it is, spread out on the ground in front of them. These are two boys guarding a chariot. This man here is a shaman. In his hand is a sacred wand. You can see similar images in European caves and across the rest of North Africa. There are even echoes of such a magician in aboriginal paintings in Australia.'

I looked closely. 'It could be a rearing animal,' I suggested, 'some kind of deer, perhaps. And even if it was a man there's nothing to prove he was a magician. Or that the thing is his hand is a wand.' I hesitated. 'It could be a club of some kind,' I added quickly.

Pryce shook his head in excitement. 'That's no club, and he's much more than just an ordinary magician. A shaman could tap into the psychic energies that thread their way through the entire universe. He had many powers. He knew how to transcend space and time. If he wanted to, he could materialise out of thin air and stand next to us now. He could even spirit us away with him, just as he spirited away my daughter.'

'Graham, I'm sorry, but none of what you say makes sense."

Quite suddenly he laughed. It was the only time I had heard him laugh, and I was taken aback for a few seconds.

'You're such a philistine,' he said. 'I've studied this. I know what I'm looking at.'

'I do too. This is evidence of a civilisation that vanished because the climate changed. And none of us know what it was. Not really.'

'You confess you don't know, and yet you doubt me?'

'You think there's something eternal about this, don't you?'

'I know it. The desert has swallowed up the water and the animals and the people, but there must still be comfort here – a kind of welcoming harmony; even a kind of perfection.'

'Do you think there are lines of power radiating out from this site, just like insane people believe there are at Glastonbury and Stonehenge?'

He nodded. 'I do. I only wish I could feel it. Lucy could. She was like that. She had an intuitive grasp of other people's true nature. She would have understood these people. She would have wanted to be with them.'

'Graham,' I said firmly.

He turned away from me quickly, as if he anticipated what I would ask.

'Graham, you think this is a kind of paradise, don't you? You think that it's somehow outside of time. That's why you want to believe that Lucy is still here.'

He turned back to me, his eyes lost beneath the reflections on the tinted lenses.

'Harmony,' he repeated, 'perfection.' He lifted his hand to a pastoral scene on the rock directly above us. 'There's the evidence. What more could anyone want?'

It was our last night at the outcrops. During the night I woke in a silence that was so infinite it seemed as if it could never be broken. The air was cold although I could sense that there was still heat stored within the sandstone towers. I looked up at the stars before I went back to sleep. For a few seconds I thought I saw something move across them, and then I realised I was so tired that my vision was slightly awry.

In the morning I woke with a start and found that Pryce had gone.

After a moment I began to panic, but then I saw his shallow footprints across sand that had drifted over a flat rock. They led towards the heart of the outcrops.

I called Pryce's name but he did not answer. And then I followed the trail until it vanished among ramps of stone.

The morning sun was striking the gulley, illuminating it so that it shone with layered pools of brightness and heat. In the cathedral Pryce stood at the bottom of a well of light, his glasses held in a hand that was hanging limply by his side. His head was craned upwards but his eyes were closed.

I approached him quietly. He did not speak but I felt sure he knew I was there.

'Graham,' I said after a while, 'we have to leave now.'

He nodded but did not move.

'I mean it,' I insisted.

'She was here,' he told me.

I felt suddenly cold, as cold as I had done when I had woken during the night.

'I could feel her presence,' he went on. 'I could feel it but I couldn't see her.'

My throat was dry. 'Did she speak?' I asked. 'Could she tell you anything?'

He shook his head. 'There were no words. But I could feel that she wants me to go back now. She must be content that we came to this place.'

I licked my lips nervously. 'That's good,' I said, my voice breaking beneath the slight weight of the words.

Pryce opened his hands. They were trembling slightly. I could see a distorted reflection of the sandstone walls in the glasses hanging from his fingers.

'It must have happened here,' he said.

'What?' I asked.

'She was singled out in some sort of way. It was only Lucy who was wanted. Someone came for her. I don't know who. I would never have recognised him.'

I leaned forward and took him by the elbow. I wondered if he could feel how much I was shaking.

'Come on.' I said; 'it's time for us to leave.'

I sit at my table in the café, smoking my kif, with Pryce's new book beside me. He has dedicated it to me, and underneath my name are the words guide, companion, friend. His narrative has transformed our journey into a kind of phantasmagoria, a pilgrim's progress towards his own enlightenment.

Perhaps, I think, some readers of this book will be moved and transformed by the mystery of Lucy's disappearance. Others will dream of visiting the shrine of the vanished explorer. Perhaps they will even employ me to take them to the outcrops and, in return, I will portray what has happened in a detailed, evocative tale of half-truths and lies.

For a while the kif makes me pleasantly drowsy. Around me all of time collapses. For a few seconds, or perhaps an hour, I dream that a kind of paradise intertwines with my surroundings. A warm sun shines beside the light-bulbs, rich grass grows across the café floor, and somewhere in the background, unlocatable but distinct, a fall of pure water cascades on smooth, cool stones.

When the experience is over I am dry-mouthed, tired, and resentful. I place the book in my bag and walk out of the café onto the dirty streets.

The tall beggar is walking towards me, alms tin in his hand, led by his daughter. He stumbles forward but does not lessen his pace. He is certain and kingly in his own narrowed world.

Shamed, and more guilty than I have ever felt before, I stand still as they approach. The girl nudges her father, who holds out his tin a little further. I am repulsed and fascinated by his upturned, shining, dead eyes, and watch them as I search for change in my pocket. Already the man is thanking me again and again. Finally I clutch a handful of coins and, not knowing what they are worth, drop them into the tin. The money clatters as loudly as a bribe.

I want to turn away but cannot. I look at his daughter. She gazes back with the blank, unbelieving expression of the condemned. And then, quite suddenly, she smiles as if to prove to me that she is happy.

Bloom

A s THE FERRY neared the island it slowed and turned so that its shifting mass pushed us both against the rail. Sophie allowed the force to move her body closer to mine but I edged further away. Smoke billowed from the funnel and the smell of burned fuel drifted across us as if from a nearby pyre. The guard rail was hot to the touch when I clasped it with both hands. Each week we defined larger and larger spaces around ourselves; even our hotel room had become a testing ground for a complex system of zones and allowances.

'I often wonder about my position,' Sophie admitted. 'Maybe you should allot me a number. Often I feel as if I'm in a competition.'

The other passengers were gathering their bags and talking in a language I did not understand. A new pitch to the engine's percussive racket drowned out the greedy clamour of gulls flapping at our wake. Sophie raised her voice above the din.

'Numbers, possessions, states of decay - you're used to cataloguing. It's your job. In your imagination you must have everyone categorised.'

Her tone was strung between melancholy and resentment, but I would not be drawn. Neither my past nor my future had anything to do with Sophie, but uncertainty had allowed her imagination to exaggerate both.

'We came here for a reason that has nothing to do with our disagreements,' I reminded her.

The onshore breeze tangled her hair and she pushed it back with one hand.

'Yes,' she said; 'your choice. It's always your choice.'

A black-clad waiter stood beneath the striped awning of a quayside restaurant and stared at the ferry as it swayed broadside to the jetty. In the shade behind him men leaned across tables and idly smoked cigarettes. Some clasped strings of beads in their hands. *Rembétika* music drifted from a nearby bar. I looked beyond the rows of pantiled houses and a scattering of white-painted villas to where crumbling medieval walls topped a grassy hill. I calculated that it would only take about twenty minutes of walking to reach them.

'We both want to get something positive out of this,' Sophie insisted. 'If that wasn't true we wouldn't have come away together.'

I did not answer. What she had thought of as a few days of reconciliation I had thought of as a farewell. She had read the signs but refused to accept their meaning. Only a few weeks ago she had talked about starting a family. I had insisted the notion was absurd. Sophie had taken that, not as a comment on the decay of our own relationship, but as the emotional consequence of my having seen too many dead children. We had already been together too long.

The ferry bumped heavily to its mooring and a metal

gangplank grated on the stone. We stood back while the other passengers disembarked and then walked down it. The gangplank flexed slightly beneath our feet. Sophie clasped my hand for stability and did not let go when we stood on the land. I was uncomfortable. Habit still allowed some everyday familiarities, but not this one.

Along the quayside we slowed to an awkward halt and found ourselves staring into the water. All the boats had been painted with bright charms against the evil eye. Beneath their keels shoals of fish moved placidly through the dappled shallows, their fins moving only slightly, their skins patterned in shades of sleek grey. Across the greenish stone of the harbour floor anemones were scattered like patches of black fur.

The waiter swilled water from the front of the restaurant and then brushed it away. Almost immediately it began to evaporate in the heat, the vapour shimmering in waves above the stone.

'I'm not certain how long I'll be away,' I said, extricating my hand so that I could adjust my rucksack. 'It'll be at least three months.' I gave a small self-deprecating laugh. 'There's no one else as good.'

'I'll wait.'

'I don't expect that.'

'Your other lovers must have given up more easily than I will.'

'It's the life I have to live. You know how important it is. I can't expect anyone to wait for me. This is the real world, not a daydream.'

A kind of desperation touched Sophie.

'I'd get used to waiting,' she insisted. 'That time when

I said I could smell death off your hands – it wasn't true. I couldn't help imagining things. Just like I can't help imagining you with women you've never told me about.'

I did not yet have the determination to be brutal so I merely looked away.

Beneath the restaurant awning a glass tank full of captive fish had been set at chest height. It was far too small for its contents and algae had smeared the inner surfaces an oily green. The captive fish circled around and around each other in blank desperation, their scales dulled with fungal growth but their eyes still bright as targets. The waiter held a long steel skewer across his chest and peered into the tank with a bored expression. He studied its contents for a few seconds and then turned away, tapping the skewer against his side.

'That seems cruel,' Sophie said.

'Maybe.'

'Poor things. They don't know what's going to happen.'

'Listen; we said we'd climb to the monastery while it's still open. Are you coming - or do you want to stay here?'

'Of course I'll come. I said I'd do that. It's important that we still do things together, don't you think?'

We began to walk at a pace that was so studied that we must both have recognised its artificiality. It was though we both feared that to break step would be to display a lack of resolve.

A stone path sloped upward between the houses and emerged on the hillside amongst villas whose walls blazed white in the sun. Above the buildings the path became packed earth, threading its way upward through gorse and withered turf. When the way grew even steeper I glanced back at the harbour. The ferry was sailing back across a sparkling sea and the blue line of the mainland stretched along the length of the horizon. Sophie spoke again.

'Last night you shouted out in your sleep. Your cries were so loud I thought the hotel would send someone to investigate.'

'I don't have nightmares.' It was a lie. My work was so harrowing that there were bound to be invasions into the nonsense world of sleep. 'Maybe you were the one who was having the bad dream,' I suggested.

'You know I haven't imagined it. It wasn't me who was terrified. Admit it, your work is harming you.'

'Archaeology isn't a harmful profession.'

'I know you believe that what you do is essential— '

'Of course it is. There can't be any argument about that.'

'— but it's work that's eating away at you in ways that you won't admit. Eventually you'll not have any humanity left. I even worry that maybe that will be the only way for you to stay sane.'

We neared the entrance to the monastery.

'My work is about justice, not about dreams,' I told her.

Fissures snaked through the monastery walls and moraines of fallen stone lay at irregular intervals along its base. To one side of a damaged arch there was a heap of masonry that had evidently come away only recently. Basking lizards disappeared swiftly into the gaps.

I looked round. 'This needs care,' I said.

We entered a deserted courtyard strewn with rubble. Incongruously, a line of washing was strung between the entrance and an olive tree in the centre of the yard. We had to step round white bedsheets before we could see the door to the building.

An expressionless old woman with mottled skin, black clothes and hair the colour of frost stared at us from a red plastic seat. In one bony hand she held a short white stick, like a wand. The other hand was thrust inside the pocket of her dress. I wondered about the history she must have seen.

Nothing happened for several seconds. I reached for the phrase book I had packed in a rucksack pocket. Before I could get it the old woman rose from her seat and took a large brass key from her apron. It turned the lock with a noise like a rifle bolt being drawn.

The wooden door seemed too heavy, but she pushed it inwards and a harsh grinding squeal echoed within the dim interior. Daylight faded on the worn bare stones just inside the doorway. As she stepped inside her heavy shoes made a clicking sound on the floor. We followed as if entering a prison cell.

Two low-wattage bulbs hung from the ceiling in a tracery of cobwebs and the suddenly chill air smelled of mould and rotted plaster.

Gradually the shape and dimensions of the room became clear. It was a barrel vault, blind at one end and with a chapel to either side. The chapel floors were littered with stones and fallen plaster. But I had come to see the narthex, and that had remained secure. Every square inch, including the ceiling, was covered by images whose colour and detail blurred and faded into darkness.

The woman transcribed an arc across the walls with her stick and announced something we could not understand.

I thought she could have been doing this for fifty or sixty years.

Staring into the gloom gave me a tugging, pressurised sensation at the outer corners of my eyes. I took two small torches from my rucksack and handed one to Sophie. She took it from me without a word.

'Twelfth century,' I said, my voice coarsened by the shape and emptiness of the vault. 'Look up there.'

We directed the beams onto the frescoes.

At the far end of the sanctuary a painted figure raised one hand in judgement. His beard and eyes were an impenetrable black, but spots of mould had spread across skin that had once been as white as the belly of an upturned fish. Behind his head was a halo of gold that gleamed against a thick swirl of fungal mottling.

I turned to Sophie, for once seeking her agreement.

'Look - the pigmentation is being eaten away. Unless this is recorded and preserved soon there will be nothing left to prove that it ever existed.'

'But it's all been written about.'

'I mean hard empirical evidence. Evidence assembled and collated by experts. Photographs. Pigment samples. Measurements. Data that no one could question.'

We swept the lights across more images. Many had faded, some were no longer decipherable, and all had begun to disintegrate. The rot was turning an entire section into unreadable abstraction; in another, human figures were losing definition and merging into a stylised landscape. If I had brushed my hand across the surface it would have come away pocked with flecks of paint.

Now the beam from Sophie's torch illuminated a wide

area near the floor that so far had escaped the bloom of decay.

In a landscape of flattened perspective, tombs and graves lay thrown open as easily as if their seals had been hinged doors. The dead erupted from their resting-places, winding sheets still wrapped around their bodies, faces upturned and hands clasped in prayer. They ascended toward heaven like flights of doves. Above them angels with opened wings were poised in welcome on a cloudless blue sky. The resurrected dead showed no emotion as they rose higher. It was as if what was happening had always been expected. Every risen soul had the curious inflexible calm of an icon.

Sophie retreated towards the doorway.

'Is this the real reason why you came?' she asked, but I would not answer.

I paced the walls for a few more minutes, studying the patterns in the decomposing imagery, and then I stepped closer to the scenes of resurrection.

The old woman held out her stick between my body and the wall. As it protruded from its black cotton sleeve her arm appeared to be nothing but skin and bone.

I lifted my hands to indicate that I had not intended to touch. The woman's rapid accusatory voice crackled like burning twigs.

'It's all right,' I told her.

'She wants us to leave,' Sophie said.

I stared at the woman. Her eyes held no depth. A film of dimness lay across them. She tapped my arm with the wand and gestured at the open door.

Sophie took another step back. I had grown accustomed

to the gloom and for a brief moment the space around her seemed to flare with light.

'She wants us get out of here and I want to leave, too,' she said.

I nodded. I had seen what I wanted.

The heavy door screeched like an alarm as the old woman pulled it shut behind us. Blinking, we picked our way across the scattered stones of the courtyard. The sheets hung motionless on the line in direct sunlight. After the prison gloom of the narthex they appeared as a startling, intense, and unsullied white.

Twenty minutes late we sat on opposite sides of a restaurant table and looked out across the harbour. The shadow of the awning in front of our feet was as sharp as a border. From the kitchen came the smell of grilled food. Behind us two old men played with their beads, passing them between their fingers in a series of rhythmic clicks. Sophie was the first to speak.

'I've done my best. You didn't even try. All you did was use that painting as a kind of demonstration.'

Beside her the captive fish swam helplessly backward and forward in their tank of smeared glass.

'I thought I would wait until you came back,' she went on. 'Now I'm not so sure.'

I knew that Sophie wanted me to ask her to stay, but I wanted her to leave. Our time together was over. I needed to get back to something that mattered.

'You have your own life and I have mine,' I said carefully. 'Yours is comfortable and mine is too important to turn away from. We should recognise that.'

We lapsed into silence until Sophie spoke again.

'How many this time?'

I shrugged. 'They think at least sixty, maybe more.'

'They don't know?'

'It's impossible to know the true number until you've finished digging. They were probably all killed in sequence on the same day. The exhumation will take a long time. The evidence is fragile.'

A low wave passed across the shimmering water and jostled the fishing boats together.

'Forensics is your work now,' Sophie said after a few seconds. 'It's a long time since you've been an ordinary archaeologist. You should call yourself something else.'

'I use the same skills and with the same end – to describe what happened.'

'Archaeologists don't dig up corpses that still have ticking watches on their wrists. They don't find bodies with hospital drip feeds still attached. They don't exhume skeletons of children with bullet holes in the backs of their heads.'

'It makes no difference what we're called,' I answered quietly, 'what matters is what we do. And that matters more than anything else that has ever touched me.'

The fishing boats thumped together and then slid apart.

'You don't really connect with real people, do you?' Sophie asked.

'I try,' I answered; 'you don't know how hard I try.'

'But you're not very successful. To you, the dead are more important than the living.'

Yes, I thought, she was right. The dead were people I

could understand. They were definable. I had no trouble with the dead.

The waiter strode from the back of restaurant, leaned over the glass tank, and skewered one of the fish. As he lifted it out the fish thrashed wildly on its spike, showering large drops across the ground in front of the awning. It was still convulsing as the waiter carried it away.

The sun beat relentlessly on the stone. It was so hot that the water was already drying. In less than a minute all of the drops would have vanished.

Junction

I RECOGNISED HIM soon as I saw him. The haircut, the clothes, even the walk were what I had expected. From the way he approached my park bench, however, it was clear that he was unconvinced about our meeting. Perhaps he was still wondering exactly who I was, what I wanted, and even why he had agreed to see me.

'I think you must be . . .' he began, and deliberately let the sentence tail off as though challenging me to finish it. I thought that its completion was unnecessary. Not to show surprise should have been recognition enough.

'Maybe we should shake hands,' I suggested.

'I don't think I want to touch you.'

A refusal was not unexpected as I'd had my own doubts, but his brusqueness was unsettling.

I had chosen to sit at one end of the bench so I raised a hand to indicate the unoccupied area to my left. For a few seconds I wondered if he was going to remain standing. Possibly he would even turn and walk away, and I decided that I could not blame him if he did. So I tried reassurance.

'I'm not going to do anything stupid. I already know that you don't.'

But he was unable to hold my gaze and instead stared out across the park. His face looked eerily young. I spoke again.

'In the time I've been allowed here I've often sat on this bench and thought about things.'

'Things in the past, you mean?'

'Not always.'

For a moment I believed I was speaking the truth, but then I realised that almost all my conscious time was taken up trying to recall a life whose details sometimes eluded my grasp. But despite my imperfect recollections I had no doubt about the shaping, defining power of the past. Clearly it had not been either intellectual or ethical determinants that had made me who I was, but actual events. How I had acted must always have been more important than what I had believed.

After a few more seconds my visitor reluctantly sat down at the far end of the bench. As though ready to stand up again at any moment he leaned slightly forward as he looked across the springtime trees, daffodils, new grass and the shining pond with its chattering ducks. I wanted to reach out and touch his hair, but knew that I should not.

'This is the first time I've visited this park,' he said.

'I've sat here for days,' I told him, although I was not sure if that was true.

The bench was fixed on top of a slight rise overlooking the arterial pathways. Despite the sunlight the air was slightly chill. Passing below us, and only occasionally glancing upwards, were dog walkers, office workers taking short cuts, and friends meeting by arrangement. There was enough space on the bench for two more people, and

I wondered what would happen if one of those strangers should unexpectedly walk up the rise and chance sitting between us. Perhaps I would be recognised. Silent and with my eyes down I had sometimes walked among these people and listened to their conversations.

Although I was unable to look away from him, my visitor still did not want to look back at me. Perhaps he believed my intention was to exploit him. The thought unsettled me, as though I should question my own motives.

I cleared my throat, aware that it was a sign of nervousness, and spoke again.

'You're a little late. Not that clock time matters. Not now.'

'I'd have been here as agreed if it wasn't for all the traffic.'

I believed him. Before he arrived I had walked to the park gates and seen that the road was busy.

'Of course you were always punctual,' I told him.

'I try to keep my promises. And if you're telling the truth then you must have known that I wouldn't let you down.'

A passer-by threw some grain to the ducks and for several seconds their demanding, slightly absurd quacks carried sharply across the park.

'I tried to ring you back but my phone hadn't registered your number,' he continued. 'Because of that I thought your call might not have actually happened. It seemed possible that I'd dreamed our conversation. For a while I wasn't convinced it had actually taken place.'

'Your number was easily remembered,' I said, although

I could not quite recollect how I had rung him. I just knew we had agreed to meet.

'Maybe I'll look back on this as happening at a different time and in a different place, maybe even in another country,' he said. 'You must know that memory can never be trusted. It betrays us too often. It could be betraying me now.'

'I can assure to you that it's not.'

And then he turned and looked me straight in the face.

'You're a lot older than I expected. And you don't look well. Are you ill?'

'My health has been better,' I admitted. 'Maybe I was given this chance because I haven't got long left. But I can't know that.'

'Are you looking for sympathy?'

'At my age sympathy is of little value.'

'And I didn't expect you to be wearing glasses. How long ago did that happen?'

'I've worn them for several years. I need them now, just like I need this hat to keep my head warm.'

'You've lost your hair?'

'That was a long time ago, too. You hope these things aren't going to happen but they do.'

He shrugged. Old age meant little to him.

'I wasn't surprised when I saw you,' I told him. 'You're exactly what I expected.'

'I'm sorry I couldn't be more of a surprise.'

'I haven't forgotten anything important about you – how could I? And if sometimes my recollections aren't as sharp as they could be then I can look at the photographs.'

'You've kept them?'

'What else would I do with photographs?'

'Even the ones that were taken later than this?'

'All of them.'

'I don't know if I want to see those. I don't think I should.'

'Even if I had them with me I'd refuse to show them. There are some things you shouldn't know.'

'Are you expecting me to ask?'

'I think you're too clever for that.'

'And I think that's the kind of assumption that you shouldn't make.'

Two joggers ran along the path below us, their breath laboured, their shoes slapping on the asphalt.

'I don't even know what to call you,' he admitted. 'I think I'd feel better if I didn't call you by name.'

'If that's what you've decided then I have to accept it. But I'll always think of you as Kenny.'

"If that's what you want. But I can't think of you as anything.'

For a few seconds I felt unreal. I knew that if he spoke my name it would somehow anchor my existence.

'This can't happen, can it?' he asked. 'Common sense is against it. The laws are against it.'

'But it *is* happening.'

'Is it?"

'Kenny, we both know that it is. Whatever the laws are, they haven't prevented our meeting. They've enabled it.'

Repeating his name was like an intake of oxygen; it re-established my sense of control.

'What you're arguing is that we can trust what's going on,' he said. 'But I can't stop wondering if everything around us actually exists. Maybe I'm hallucinating. It's as if somehow I've been able to walk into a mirage, and all this is a fantasy, a deception.'

I wanted to grasp him by the shoulder but resisted. It would have been good to touch him.

'Listen to me,' I insisted. 'We're talking to each other on a bench in a park. We can feel how solid it is beneath our weight. This whole area has spatial coordinates; you can check what they are. Living, breathing people are walking along the paths and there are ducks on the pond that we can hear as well as see. It's chilly even though the sun is shining. The daffodils are out. It's spring. All of these things are real. They're not false.'

'How can you be so certain?'

'Kenny, I've had more time to adjust than you have. I've thought all of this through. Over the last few days I've been able to come to terms with the opportunity and be grateful for it.'

'If that's the case then you must know what you want out of this—' He considered a moment before completing his sentence. 'Trick world,' he said.

'I didn't want anything other than to meet you. I was given that chance. That's all. No one would refuse an offer like that.'

'You're content just to be here?'

It was true, and I nodded.

'But I don't know what you expect of me,' Kenny said. 'You don't appear to be anything distinctive; you just seem to be an old man who needs to be reminded of his own youth. Is that why I'm here? I hope that watching me makes you happy, because I don't like looking at you. It disturbs me too much. All I'm getting out of this encounter is uncertainty and a kind of fear. Nothing in my world is stable anymore.'

'Give our meeting a chance and you'll soon see its value.'

'You act as if you know everything, but I can't be certain that you do. Maybe you actually know nothing. Maybe all this is just a ruse. We both know that there's a way of proving that it's real but it seems that you don't want me to ask. Exactly how much can you tell me about what happens after this?'

I could understand why he challenged me, but I still found it annoying. The irritation came through in my answer.

'Not only can I *not* tell you such things, I know that I *don't* tell you them.'

'That sounds as if you actually have no idea what's going to happen.'

I shook my head and he leaned forward a little. It was the closest we had been to each other.

'Why don't you make something up?' he suggested. 'That could be the way to convince me. After all, what would it matter? If you invented an untruth it would become as insubstantial as a dream. When its time came I would go on living my life completely unaffected.'

And I began to wonder what I could say to Kenny that would convince him and yet have no consequences on his life and therefore on mine.

'We both know you don't want to be told a lie,' I reasoned. 'You need me to tell you something that will actually happen. You must see it as a matter of trust.'

'I'd like to see it as a prophecy.'

'I already know I don't tell you anything important. You must realise why.'

He thought for a few seconds and then continued.

'It would depress me to think that I never got out of this town.'

I said nothing. He appeared to be considering possibilities.

'Travel will be a safe subject. It has no dangers. Just like thousands of others, I must go abroad, even if only for holidays. Tell me about some of the countries that I visit.'

Immediately a series of vivid but unconnected images flickered in either my memory or my imagination; I was not sure which. They were motionless but colourful, like photographs of landscapes and buildings glimpsed in a guidebook held in the hand but skimmed through with neither engagement nor interest. And yet I was convinced that my travels had been both varied and rich, and that afterwards I had often entertained my friends with anecdotes about them – although for the moment the names of those friends escaped me.

'Yes,' I said, 'I'm sure you'll travel. Given the chance, most people do.'

It was an evasion and he recognised it as such.

'If you won't even tell me which countries I visit,' he said, 'then there's no chance you'll tell me about my love affairs, is there? Tell me if there is.'

'I remember that I refuse to answer that question.'

'It wouldn't bother me if your answers were so generalised and unspecific that they turned out to be worthless. I just want to know that I can look forward to some excitement. God knows I haven't had much so far.'

Yes, I thought: I've had good times; intense times. And even though I could tell him nothing I began to revisit my relationships and assignations. The memories were layered and vivid, but as I tried to recover the specifics they became shallow and inauthentic. Unexpectedly my passions had become carnivalesque, like the products of a dreaming mind. Even the settings, the décor and the beautiful compliant women belonged not to reality but to elaborately staged masques. I was not even sure of my own identity within them.

I shook my head. The memories were unreal, perhaps even implanted. A chill like the touch of a knife ran through me as I understood at last that amnesia was eating ever more rapidly and deeply into my past.

Kenny became aggressive.

'You look puzzled,' he said. 'Can't you remember what happened? I'm sure I wouldn't have forgotten about love affairs.'

'That kind of knowledge would wreck your future and my past. We couldn't even be certain that I'd still be living.'

He considered for a moment.

'In that case I'll ask you a very simple everyday question.'

'Kenny, you have to stop this. Think of all the paradoxes it could throw up.'

'The answer will be either yes or a no; all right?'

'I don't know. Maybe.'

'The question is this – do I marry? I don't need any other details. I don't even want names. I just want to know if I ever get married; yes or no.'

And I thought that perhaps I could, without harm,

give him an answer that wouldn't really matter. I need not disclose any identities, professions, families or geography. I could be discreet to the point of secrecy.

Then, shockingly, I realised that I no longer knew what the answer was.

Only a few seconds ago I had known – or could have sworn that I had known – and yet suddenly lives other than my own were no longer reachable. I did not know if I had ever had a wife or wives. Whoever she had been, or whoever they were, had withdrawn into a darkened corner of my mind where even their outlines were no longer legible.

A sense of panic swept through me as I became momentarily incapable of thinking. Perhaps all such details were being scoured from my consciousness. Soon I would be helpless, stranded, and bereft of personality. Only after a few seconds did I realise that at least some of the essential elements of the self were still functioning, because I knew who I was and why I was there.

'I can't tell you that,' I said.

Kenny was staring hard at me. 'You mean you refuse to tell me.'

'I don't know the answer,' I confessed. 'I can't remember what happened. The memories are gone. Kenny, I'm not lying.'

And it seemed to me that I stood in the shallows of a vast fathomless lake of forgetfulness, and that in a few more steps the blackness would close over my head completely and forever.

Kenny became scornful. 'This meeting has been a fiasco. I should never have agreed to it. Whoever you are, you're a fraud and a liar. You have nothing to do with me. I was a fool to think you might have.'

Even though I could no longer remember any of the women I had loved, his rejection seemed more wounding than that of any lover. As he stood up I held out my hand in an appeal, but he was too quick and within a few paces was standing out of reach.

'I'm going,' he said. 'Don't call me back.'

I did not know how to prevent him. I hadn't remembered him leaving so quickly. Or maybe I had forgotten that, too.

'Please don't go,' I pleaded. 'Seeing my youth again means everything to me.'

Kenny took three steps farther away but he was still looking at me.

"There's something wrong with you,' he said. 'You need treatment. Have you been stalking me? If you have, you've got to stop it now.'

A sense of despair grew within me. The failure hadn't been entirely my fault. Kenny had simply refused to accept the limitations on what I was able to say.

'Why would I lie to you?' I asked. 'We're the same person. In a few more decades you'll look in the mirror and find my face looking back at you. I can already see it in your expression now.'

But he turned and began to walk away. For a moment I considered pursuit, but I knew that could only exacerbate our problems, so I called after him.

'Think it over. We should talk some more.'

And then, when he neither turned nor broke step, I shouted again.

'I'll be here tomorrow. Meet me tomorrow.'

It was too loud. I glanced at other visitors walking through the park, but no one turned their heads and neither did Kenny. In a few more paces he reached the gate and then disappeared beyond it into the ordinary world of streets and traffic and his youth.

When I looked down I saw that my hands were spread out, almost as if they could grasp all our hopes and all our paradoxes and hold them close until Kenny and I could meet again.

It was the last time I saw him.

Because there are no other choices I still wait at the bench during the hours of daylight. It is unclear where I go to at night. Meanwhile the life of the park continues uninterrupted on the paths and lawns and along the edge of the pond. For those visitors everything is normal, but to me my presence has become hopeless, as if I were an old forgotten soldier guarding an abandoned post. I also know that I am changing in frightening ways over which I have no control. Recently my hand has become almost translucent, and if I hold it up to the light it seems to be made not of flesh and bone but of something resembling melting ice. Even my clothes are losing their colours and degrading into an undifferentiated grey.

A few days ago a young couple came to sit on my bench. They were so absorbed in each other that I decided they had not noticed me and were about to rest on my part of the seat. I stood up, moved to one side, and tried to say that they should look where they were going. Momentarily puzzled, the woman glanced round, did not notice me, and then looked back at her companion. Suddenly I realised that I could not be seen and that if I was heard it had only been very faintly.

Later I began to understand that I have become invisible to everyone in the park, and that whenever I speak my words will be distant and indistinguishable, as if hailed from the limit of audibility. Perhaps I should have expected this. I had believed myself to be a messenger from the future, but now I have to think of myself as a consequence of the past. I am not truly real, and my presence clings to the outermost edge of existence.

Of course such beliefs are persuasive indicators of madness. It may be that it I am the one who inhabits a trick world, and no one else. Perhaps nothing I have described so far has been empirically true. What I subsequently learned about Kenny would necessarily be part of that illusion, and yet I cannot accept such a conjecture.

For the sake of my own sanity I am convinced that several days ago I sat on this park bench and talked to my younger self. I must have no doubts about this.

I cannot tell, however, how long I will be able to continue waiting here. There is little point to my vigil because it is impossible that the two of us will ever meet again. Whatever our time together was, it ended as brutally as if it had been cut by a knife.

A little later than our meeting, or possibly just before, Kenny was killed at a road junction just outside the gates. For the rest of that day and part of the next, the park visitors exchanged the news excitedly, as though they had personally witnessed the accident.

His death has consequences. The most obvious one is

that in any normal sense I cannot be alive. When Kenny was killed his future must necessarily have died too. My past was obliterated at the same time as his life, so it is impossible that he grew into the older man I believe myself to be. And if I am not a Kenny grown older and wiser, then I must be something else.

After brooding hard on the paradox I have now reached a rational conclusion.

I must have been created as a kind of hypothesis. As Kenny lived out his everyday youth he conjured a counterlife from speculation and invention: I am that other life, somehow given duration and presence. But his dreamed futures cannot have been imagined either rigorously or systematically, as I have been equipped with both memories and fantasies that are facile and without texture. Sometimes they are little more than categories. My inability to remember was not my own failure, but that of my younger self. Kenny must have been like a writer scribbling chapter headings for a memoir he would never complete.

I am not a person; I am not even a simulacrum. I am a wraith, an invention, an immaterial and unobservable intrusion in a world of measurable substance.

And I must also acknowledge that there is another interpretation. It is even worse than insanity but I am unable to ignore it. One can recover from madness, but not from the possibility that Kenny released me into the world only in the final moments before he died. Perhaps, at this very instant, I have actually been aware for only a few moments, and that what I now experience as slowly passing days are but fractions of a second.

It could be that I never met Kenny at all. Perhaps I merely imagined him as he failed to reconcile himself, not with a future he had lost, but with a future that had never belonged to him. Maybe the park, its people, my presence, and even my thoughts exist within a constricted moment of time, scarcely longer than the drawing of a final breath. I am distinctive, unique, a singularity who cannot judge if a few seconds have passed or an entire year, and who assures himself that he is alive but secretly knows that he cannot be.

At first I was scared but I have learned to accept whatever my fate will be. And if I sense that time is passing, I have to believe that it actually passes at the speed at which I witness it. I am unseen, unheard, and alone, but whatever my physical state there is a core to me that remains human. I will continue to honour that even as I accept that I do not know what my future has to be.

There is little left of me. Perhaps I will merely fade away, like a lamp that imperceptibly wanes until it holds the merest hint of illumination. What will be left of me then – a disturbance in the vision of passers-by, as if the atmosphere had somehow momentarily warped? Or will I be a scarcely audible whisper that only some are able to hear but not understand, and the reason that they will turn to their bewildered companions to ask if they heard a noise like someone breathing?

I stand guard by the bench as a cloud darkens the grass in the park. A breeze troubles the surface of the pond. My body and even my clothes seem no longer to be material, but composed of fog. If I put my hand on my chest the skin offers no resistance. I feel that my fingers could flow into my ribs like a stream of mist. The air temperature dips and it begins to drizzle.

I cannot feel the raindrops as they pass through my body and fall on the ground beneath me.

A Visit to the Bonesetter

THE DEPARTMENT DOESN'T just print the original summons; it makes copies for everyone living at the same address. Only the very young are exempt, so that details may even be read by school children. We are told that the system remains highly efficient because annual censuses ensure that there can be only marginal deviations from government occupancy records.

So much is known about us that the instructions could easily be issued online, but officials believe that old-fashioned protocols add an extra layer of authority. These procedures also foster surprise and unease, as it is considered politically advantageous for neighbours to watch the distinctively uniformed agents as they stride up to selected doors.

Deliveries follow an identical course. A summons is served to the person named on the document, and they are also given copies that they must pass to the other residents. If no one answers the knock then the envelopes are not posted through the letterbox but taped to the outside of the door, this arrangement being photographed as proof of delivery. This image is then transmitted by phone as a confirmation. It is the only communication that is ever sent by phone.

Of course everyone is concerned that they could be the next to receive a summons. Although statistically the chances of that happening are not high, a concern about its arrival runs through every street, every family, and every home. This is why even before I answered the unexpected knock I had begun to imagine the delivery agents. And as soon as I opened the door I saw that it was them.

A man and woman stood outside. They both carried shoulder bags. The man held two envelopes, one white and one brown. The woman stood behind him with a clipboard. Cameras like giant black beetles were fixed to the lapels of their uniforms.

I did not know if they wanted me or Lisa. Even as our future hung in the balance I had the tangential thought that I was pleased that we didn't have children.

As though assessing my capacity to make trouble, the delivery man briefly looked me up and down before asking if my name was Keith Smith.

'Is it my name on the white one?' I asked.

'I don't think I need repeat my question,' he said, and I knew I must formally tell him what he wanted to know. At the same time my wife called from down the corridor that led to the back of the house.

'I'm Keith Smith,' I said. 'Am I the person that you want?'

The delivery man leaned forward so that he could peer down the corridor. Lisa took a few hesitant steps towards us. I wondered if he found her attractive.

'Is your name Lisa Smith?'

'Yes.'

'Mrs Smith, I need you to stand here in front of me. We're not allowed to enter property unless there are special circumstances.'

Such as severe disability, I thought, but was cautious enough to remain silent. Lisa came to stand slightly behind me and to one side, as though I could shield her.

'Mrs Smith, I am required by law to hand you this demand to present yourself to our official bonesetter. Your appointment is next Tuesday at two in the afternoon. All relevant details are given in a document in the white envelope that you must now take from me. I shall also hand you a copy for your husband. This is contained in the brown envelope that you must by law pass to him. In case you need assistance after your session it will be necessary for you to take a companion with you. In your case it must be your husband.'

He handed both envelopes to Lisa. Almost immediately, as if fearing infection, she passed the brown one to me. 'Will you come with me?' she asked.

'You know I will.'

The delivery woman stepped forward and extended her clipboard. 'I need your signature, Mrs Smith,' she said in an unexpectedly kindly voice. 'I have a pen.' And then she anticipated my next question. 'Only the prime recipient needs sign.'

I watched Lisa's hand tremble as she began to write her name. 'Does it have to be next Tuesday?' she asked.

The man answered. 'If you wish you may apply for a deferment, but I must inform you that such requests are seldom granted. Do you have hospital treatment on that day, or an appointment with a government officer?'

Lisa shook her head. The man said nothing further because he did not have to, but as soon as she had retrieved the clipboard the woman spoke again.

'I wouldn't worry too much, Mrs Smith. It's like every examination; most patients just want to get it over with. It's not usually as bad as they imagine.'

I touched Lisa's arm very lightly to stop her saying more but she ignored me. 'People on the street—'

The woman interrupted. 'Recipients are instructed never to discuss their appointments outside the home, so your so-called people on the street feel they have to invent things. You should take no notice. Almost everyone who is summonsed finds it a positive experience. And afterwards they can relax; most are unlikely to be summonsed again for several years.'

'Each month we read the statistics,' the man explained. 'It's part of the job. The bonesetter encourages his patients to respond and their answers are tabulated. Most say they were glad that they were chosen.'

'Are those answers given anonymously?' Lisa asked.

'Of course not,' the woman said. 'We need to keep track of our citizens. Maybe you'd be surprised by their comments. Some patients say that it's as satisfying as a therapy session or a confession. It makes them feel good about themselves. They see it as a form of catharsis.' She spoke the last word as if she had just been taught it.

Her companion was eager to leave. 'We have more envelopes to deliver.'

'Do you usually say to other people what you've just said to me?' Lisa asked.

'We can't tell you that,' he said.

They formally extended their hands and we shook them, although neither of us wanted to. As soon as they had gone Lisa turned and put her arms round me. We were both still holding our unopened envelopes.

'You'll get through this,' I said. It was the kind of thing I thought I should say.

'That woman said *not usually*: she didn't say *never*.'

'You shouldn't read too much into that sort of comment.'

'She made it quite deliberately. They've been schooled in what to say.'

We walked to our living room and sat opposite each other. For a few seconds I held my envelope between my hands as if somehow I could assess the contents merely by its texture and weight. Before I could open it Lisa began to open hers. It was sealed so firmly that it took several seconds before she could withdraw the document. The summons was formal, legal, bureaucratic, and minimal. Beneath her personal details was a requirement that she present herself for an examination at our local bonesetting centre on the following Tuesday afternoon at 2.00.

I opened mine. All my details were quoted correctly, and the text notified me that my wife had been selected for examination. The date and time were confirmed.

Lisa shook her head. 'I don't know why we put up with this,' she said. 'It's cruel.'

'People voted for social control. It was in the manifesto.'

'I didn't vote for the bonesetters, just like I didn't vote for a yearly census or labour camps or the emergency laws. If we were able to vote again—'

'They say that eventually that'll be allowed.'

'They're lying. And why did they pick me? I've done nothing wrong. Why didn't they pick *you*?'

'Lisa, it has nothing to do with choice. You know it hasn't. Everyone's details are fed into a machine. It's random. Your name and mine had exactly the same chance of being chosen.'

'You wouldn't have been so relaxed if it had happened to you.'

There was little else that I could say. A visit to the bone-setter was not a punishment, and she knew it. It was an assertion, a measure; a levy, and a duty. It was what we had to do to maintain stability. We didn't like it, and most of us were scared of it, but we had all agreed that it was necessary.

The surgeries have all been located in areas where property prices are low. The buildings themselves are drab and undistinguished, often being converted parish halls or school annexes. A small plaque fixed next to a locked door states their function.

We announced ourselves to a security camera fixed to the wall and were told to enter by a voice that didn't sound human. The door opened and then closed behind us.

A short hallway led to a drab rectangular reception area that smelled of disinfectant. In it were several unoccupied and uncomfortable chairs and on the wall between two windows there was a notice listing the rules of attendance. The room was divided by a chest-high wooden barrier with clear plastic screens and a closed gate: Behind it was an unlit corridor flanked by two uniformed men. One was a security guard with the protective visor raised on his helmet and a riot stick hanging on a hook on the wall behind him. He was reading a magazine that appeared to be nothing but photographs. The other man was looking down at an open ledger on the desk in front of him. His uniform resembled that of a minor official and his hair was pushed back from his forehead as if he habitually smoothed it. I recognised his thin nose and colourless, ordinary face. Beside me Lisa altered her stance. She knew him, too.

'Trevor,' I said.

He looked at us as if we were strangers.

We were almost neighbours, but not friends, although we knew each other's first names. He had often walked past our house with his dog, and we had grown used to passing the time of day without ever talking about anything important. I had always assumed that Trevor was a civil servant in a government department; I had never imagined he would be an official in the bonesetter administration.

'Mrs Lisa Smith?' he asked.

'You know that's who I am,' Lisa said.

'There's a protocol here and we're all expected to follow it. So I am asking you officially – are you Mrs Lisa Smith?'

'Yes.'

'And you are Mr Keith Smith, husband of Lisa Smith?'

'I am.'

Trevor made a note in the ledger that I thought was probably just a tick.

'Mrs Smith,' he said, 'the bonesetter will be with you in a moment. Your appointment today is with Mr Jolley. He'll collect you at this gate and afterwards he'll deliver you back here. And you, Mr Smith, you must stay where you are. You're not allowed to go any farther than this barrier. Your job is to collect your wife and make sure she gets home safely.'

Formalities over, Trevor relaxed and smoothed his hair. 'I know what the two of you must be thinking— Mr *Jolley*. But he really is called that. We didn't make it up.'

'Is he—' Lisa began.

He interrupted her. 'He's one of our most experienced bonesetters. A few years ago, before the start of the programme, he was a chiropractor. He's quite an expert, our Mr Jolley. You'll be in good hands.'

Almost immediately a man in a short-sleeved white tunic appeared from the corridor behind him. He had the trimmed greying hair and broad, slightly florid face of a favourite uncle, but I could see the strength in his arms. Lisa took a tiny step backwards as he announced himself.

'I'm your bonesetter for today, Mrs Smith. My name is Mr Jolley. I know you'll be apprehensive, but I'm sure we'll get on fine.'

He reached forward and unlocked the gate. As he did so the security guard put his picture magazine to one side and stared hard at me as if he was waiting for me to make trouble. Trevor looked down at his ledger. Lisa did not move.

Mr Jolley reached forward and made a slight beckoning motion with his hand, as if he were summoning a pet animal. 'Come, now, Mrs Smith,' he coaxed her. 'It will make everything easier if you cooperate.'

'You'd better go,' I said, although we both knew she had no choice.

Lisa walked forward and Mr Jolley took her by the elbow to steer her through the gate. 'There now.' he said soothingly as he locked the gate behind them, 'let's get this over with as quickly as we can.'

He was still holding her arm as they walked down the corridor and went out of sight.

Uncertain what to do, I sat down on one of the empty chairs. The guard returned to his magazine. Trevor decided he must warn me.

'Keith, none of us will speak of this whenever we meet again. It must remain our secret.'

'I understand,' I said.

He turned a page on the ledger and then turned it back again. Everything was quiet. Several minutes passed. I looked at the poster on the wall but the words slipped from my mind as soon as I read them.

A softened grunt came from the direction of the corridor. I looked at the guard and Trevor. Neither man reacted. I heard it again.

'Don't move, Keith,' Trevor said without looking up.

After another few minutes there was a sharp gasp, a moment's silence, and then an agonised cry. I knew it must be Lisa but I had never heard her make a sound like that.

'What's going on?' I asked.

'That's not for you to know,' Trevor answered as he checked his hair. 'But if it's any consolation, I would think that the conversation is going quite well.'

'You know about these things?'

'I've worked here since we opened. I know my job. And I had to visit a bonesetter myself as part of the induction process.'

There was another cry, as if from someone wounded,

and then a noise of weeping that ended as suddenly as it had started.

'I don't know if I can stand this,' I said. The guard unhooked his riot stick from the wall but Trevor motioned him to be calm.

'Of course you can stand it,' he said. 'That's why you're here. We all want security, don't we? This is one of the ways that we achieve it.'

I got out of the seat but had enough sense not to walk towards the barrier. The guard put his fingers on the edge of his visor as though ready to lower it if I moved any closer.

There was loud piercing scream that cut through the building like the motion of a saw. I stepped back. The sudden silence vibrated as if the air pressure had peaked but was settling like a wave.

Trevor became an official again.

'I believe Mr Jolley will be finishing his examination about now. Your wife may need some assistance, Mr Smith. Please be ready to help her in whatever way is necessary.'

I walked around the chairs because I could not think of what else I could do, and then I saw movement within the corridor.

Lisa came walking unevenly out of the gloom as if each step was painful. Her head was down, her hair dishevelled, her arms hung limply by her sides, and she looked as if she had dressed too quickly. Mr Jolley was supporting her with one hand around her shoulder and the other gripping the top of her hip. His head was turned towards her and he was murmuring something into her ear.

I moved towards the gate but Trevor held up a hand to indicate I should stop. 'When we tell you,' he warned.

Mr Jolley and Lisa halted three paces short of the barrier. 'That was very good, Mrs Smith,' he said. 'You handled everything very well. Just let me help you a little more. Would you look up, please?'

Lisa raised her head. Her eyes were red and her cheeks smeared with tears but I saw no bruises. Mr Jolley reached into a pocket, pulled out a tissue, and gently dried her face. She flinched as he touched her. And then he walked her to the gate as Trevor unlocked it.

'You may take her now, Mr Smith,' he said, and passed my wife to me.

Lisa tried to stand on her own but was too exhausted. I took her weight and then adjusted my hold so that she was more secure.

'You can be proud of the way that your wife behaved,' Mr Jolley said. 'I only hope my next patient is as amenable.'

He was already turning away and within a few seconds he had vanished into the gloom of the corridor.

Lisa rested in my arms but stared at the floor as if she could not bear to raise her head.

'It's all over,' Trevor said. 'You can leave now.'

I realised that I hated Trevor but dared not say so. 'I'll not forget this.' I told him.

'No,' he said briskly, 'that's the idea.'

On the way back Lisa said nothing. Instead she just stared out of the window with a raised hand shielding her face. As soon as we reached home she went upstairs, stayed there for some time, and came back down having showered and changed all of her clothes. Then she told me that she would be moving into the spare bedroom and that if

I ever had to visit the bonesetter then I would understand why.

For a while she evaded my questions, but eventually I asked that we sit opposite each other and talk. Somehow Lisa appeared smaller, confined, her head lowered and her arms held close to her sides as if she had drawn herself in to occupy a narrower space.

I thought that the bonesetter must have interrogated her about her life, beliefs and political views. I was wrong. His questions had been so generalised and mundane that at first she could not believe there would have been any point in their keeping her answers.

'It's not about digging out sensitive information,' she explained. 'That's not what they want. Don't misunderstand me. Mr Jolley is an expert at the application of pain and distress and I would have told him anything. I'd have talked about how we live and how we voted and why we decided not to have children. I was sure he would insist on that kind of information, but he didn't want to know any secrets. His hands were invasive but the questions weren't. He didn't ask anything important.'

'He must have found out something or your visit had no purpose.'

'He asked about everyday things; ridiculous things – favourite places or songs, childhood memories, moments of happiness; events and items and anecdotes that are part of normal conversation. Everyone's session must be the same. We must all get treated in that way.'

She paused for a moment. I thought of Mr Jolley quietly asking Lisa about her childhood at the same time as his unrelenting hands were stressing her muscles to the edge of tearing, her tendons to the point of snapping, her bones to the last degree before dislocation.

'I wanted to get out as quickly as I could,' she said, 'so I told him the experience had been valuable. Everyone must say that. I thought it was a lie, but now I think it might have been true.'

'I can't see any value in what happened to you. It was just sinister and cruel.'

'And undermining – that's its purpose."

I still couldn't see it.

'Keith, a visit to the bonesetter changes everything. Now whenever I think about the best things in my life I'll only be able to think of them with Mr Jolley's hands on me. Favourite places, meals overlooking the sea, the songs we listened to when we first met, being a child, this house, my own looks and clothes and makeup, anything I was made to talk about when I was stretched out on that operating table – they're all different now. Because I can't think of them without remembering the threat and the anguish and the shame I suffered when I talked of them. My memories are ruined, and that means that my life is.'

And I thought that it must follow that my life, too, had undergone a form of ruin.

'They do it because they can do it,' I said quietly.

'Yes,' Lisa said. 'We're scared of interrogation but say that we approve because we believe it keeps us safe. They were handed that power and they'll never give it up. And don't say that I'll get over this. We both know that I won't.'

'I understand.'

She shook her head. 'You don't really. You're a good

man, Keith, but you'll have to visit the bonesetter yourself before you really understand.'

And I wondered what memories Mr Jolley would draw from me when his unavoidable hands twisted my bones and flesh into configurations that balanced on the very edge of agony and unconsciousness. What would he demand of the memories that gave my own life a history and a direction and a meaning, and which of his carefully executed contortions would make them forever associated not with pleasure but with pain?

Lisa and I sat together in silence. Our past lives were like mere shadows in the room. After a while I reached out and took her hand but she did not respond. Outside, in towns across the country and streets not far away, the delivery agents would be knocking on other doors and handing over a summons to visit the bonesetter. In five years' time, or ten, or more, they will still be doing this.

And at some point they'll come for me.

Foreigner

W HEN I RETURNED it was to a celebration fit for heroes. Banners had been hoisted across buildings, flags draped from windows, and a proud and happy country greeted every homecoming. The woman I would marry had waited for hours on a thronged quayside, and when we met we clung together so tightly that it seemed our very bones were interlinked.

That was a long time ago. And it doesn't always happen that way. Often it's different and we're escorted down a respectfully muffled street where flags are lowered in salute and mute tearful women throw single roses onto shiny black hearses.

Today I have to wait in freezing drizzle until the front door is unlocked, and then my wife and I stand looking at each other for a few seconds. My hands are pushed deep into the pockets of my combat trousers as if searching for the keys I once owned. I tell myself that I'm almost as cold as I was on that trek across the island. It would only irritate Debbie if I admit this, so I just apologise for being late.

'Is this deliberate?' she asks.

'No,' I insist. A fabricated excuse dies in my throat

because I know that she will see straight through me. It takes a few seconds before she responds.

'All right,' she says, 'but I want you out of here in thirty minutes. We have just enough time.'

I nod understandingly but I know she recognises my disdain. 'Of course,' I say; 'Vince.'

'That's right,' she answers crisply, 'Vince.'

I haven't even seen the new man in her life so I'm often troubled by curiosity and envy.

'Come on then,' she says. 'We'll get you sorted.'

Debbie opens the door further and I step inside. The house looks and smells different, and at the bottom of the stairs there's a shaded rectangle on the wallpaper where my photograph had once hung. I take off my cap and hang my coat on a hook inside the door as though I still had ownership. Increasingly I feel like an invader in what had been my home.

'You've let your hair far too long this time,' Debbie says. 'You haven't shaved either, and you don't suit stubble. When was it last cut?'

'You did it a while back. Just before we got the news.'

She nods quickly. 'I remember.'

I wonder if I should grimace or shrug or reach out my hand or perhaps even embrace her, but while I am deciding she walks quickly into the living room and I follow like an obedient dog.

A new portrait of Alex has appeared amongst the five others on the small table at one side of the room. A photograph of our wedding used to stand there alongside one of me receiving my medal. I wonder what she's done with them – put them in a suitcase under the bed, probably.

Debbie makes all her own decisions now. She's independent. My opinion is like my past – it means nothing.

Near the far window, where the light is stronger, there's a straight-backed chair. The hairdressing clippers, scissors, and comb have been placed on the table beside it. If I wanted, I could sit there and watch the recorded clip playing on the television. Men in helmets and desert camouflage are crouched behind a rough mud-brick wall. Spiky palms sprout on the far side of the wall. Gunfire crackles in the slightly unreal way that it sounds on a recording, as if a shot could cause but little harm.

'You're watching him again.'

'I can't stop,' Debbie admits. 'Anyway, I know you do the same. Do you want me to switch it off before he turns?'

'That would be wrong, wouldn't it – a kind of insult.'

She picks up the remote control in readiness.

After a few seconds Alex turns his head. I know that he is in part-profile for about the length of a slow intake of breath, and before he can turn aside Debbie pauses the recording. Alex is young, handsome, determined, and professional. With the motion frozen like that he seems like a man with a whole life ahead.

'He looks just like you used to look,' she says.

'A long time ago.'

'Yes,' she agrees, 'a long time ago.'

Debbie presses the play button again. Alex turns his face away from us and the noise of shooting resumes. She presses the off buttons. The screen goes a lifeless grey.

'Take a seat,' she instructs me, her briskness emphasising that we don't have much time. Certainly she wants me out of the way before Vince arrives.

As soon as I sit down she places a towel across my shoulders. The scissors click behind my ear as though being tested for sharpness. I remember how I was told in training that scissors jabbed with the right force in the right place could kill within seconds. At the same time I was also shown how to kill someone with a metal hairdressing comb.

The outer edge of a blade slides across the back of my neck. I have heard men killed with bayonets and will never forget the sound.

'You'll not make me look stupid, will you?'

'I've only been cutting hair for over thirty years. Look, it makes things difficult if you move. I don't *need* to do this, you know.'

'Why do it, then?'

'Because *someone* has to take care of you, that's why. You'd look like a tramp if you had your own way. What woman would think twice about you when you look like this? You're still a good-looking man, you know. Sort of. I remember when you were younger and spruced up you were really attractive. No wonder I fancied you.'

Debbie is concentrating so hard that her sentences are broken by pauses.

'And besides,' she says, 'I have to get on with the everyday things in life. So do you. That's important. That's what they tell you to do. Otherwise you'll just . . . go under.'

To steady my head she spreads her fingers firmly across my skull. I can feel their pressure. A curl of hair falls on my sleeve. It's lank and streaked with grey.

'Hold *still*. Yes, you used to be really handsome.'

'I was a different person back then.'

'We both were. Things came between us.'

'I was never unfaithful. Never.'

'Don't be stupid. I mean the wars. Your war. Alex's war. Except that they weren't your wars. Not really. They were someone else's.'

And I think again of the dead soldier stretched out on the wintry hill a cold dark ocean away. His bare head was tilted back and his unshaven jaw was thrust upwards so that each separate bristle showed dark and clear above his startlingly white throat. His left arm was crooked beside him, the other lay across his chest with its fingers grasping something within his uniform. Away in the distance a chill noiseless dawn had broken across bare hills stripped of colour.

'Whether they're our wars or someone else's, they're still worth fighting,' I insist.

The scissors pause. 'How can you say that? How can you even think it, when you lost friends and now you've lost your son?'

'Because it's the only way to make sense of things. You've got to believe in what you're doing. When we landed – '

'For God's sake, *please* don't give me another lecture on the past.'

'If the past doesn't get talked about then it gets forgotten. It'll be the same with Afghanistan and Iraq. They'll even forget Northern Ireland.'

'The Falklands ended ages ago. I'm sick of hearing about it. People don't want to listen to that stuff anymore.'

'That's the point – they *should* listen. It's what we had to do. And what we did mattered. We *won*.'

'It was worthless. All of it.'

'Not if you lived on those islands, and not if you had some idea of duty. The war was about being invaded by a foreign power. It was about people's rights and the kind of lives they want to lead. It was about their freedom.'

Debbie used to believe that too, but I can feel her tense up as if I've spoken the biggest lie of all.

'You think that freedom is what all wars are about,' she says flatly.

'Isn't it obvious?'

'Not to me. Not to other mothers. Alex didn't die for our freedom or anyone else's. There was nothing noble about the way he was sacrificed. I don't think he helped protect us here in the West. And let's face it, everything out there is backward and repressive and corrupt. We're not achieving anything by fighting and dying in that country.'

But I believe that we are. I believe that if we weren't there then people's lives would be so tormented they would be impossible.

'His death was pointless,' Debbie insists.

As though it is necessary to look Alex in the face as she speaks, she turns to study the photos on the table.

At the front of the display is a portrait of Alex in his uniform. He stands between us looking proud and happy. He knows he has made the right choice. His parents are proud, too, but although there is nothing hidden in my own face Debbie is unable to fully disguise her doubt. Even back then she was never persuaded that Alex had done the right thing.

'He was just in the wrong place at the wrong time,' she goes on, and her voice begins to shake. 'He shouldn't even have *been* out there. Whoever killed him did it from a distance. His murderer didn't look him in the eye. He didn't *choose* Alex. He won't have bad dreams about him. He didn't even know what Alex looked like.'

I say nothing.

'And when he was brought back, when he came back home, we weren't even allowed to see him.'

'It was maybe just as well.'

'I *know* that. But I wanted to. I *wanted* to.'

I do not answer. We both know that our son was scarcely recognisable.

Although we lived apart by then, Debbie and I had agreed that we should be together when Alex's personal possessions were returned. Every one of them felt like a blow.

There was a surprise among them. Alex's girlfriend had left him three months before he was killed and had not even attended his funeral, and yet we discovered that he still kept her photograph in his wallet. By then he must have meant nothing to her. Quite probably she had destroyed or hidden every image she had of him, and yet Alex still carried her portrait close to his heart. I had looked at her face for a long time. Everything I touched was a message from the past.

In my own war I had seen an enemy soldier turned into a crackling torch by an incendiary flare. He ran direction-less and screaming, the blaze illuminating a ramshackle barricade until at last he collapsed. When we rushed forward his limbs were still thrashing and the sodden turf steamed around his body. The grey dawn smelled of peat and burned hair and phosphorus, but all sounds dropped beneath the heavy madness in my heart. Some of the men we bayoneted in the dugout. Others scrambled from it and fled. I followed one as he stumbled wildly across the bleak dark hill. His unfastened helmet toppled from his head and his coat flapped weakly around him like the wings of an injured bird. There was smoke in my throat and dying shrieks in my ears. I stopped and took aim. The man was in my sights. There was no escape. I knew I had him.

And suddenly he stopped and threw down his rifle, almost as if he had rehearsed the moment. It hit the turf with a curious flat motion. And then he turned and looked at me with wide, fearful eyes and an unshaven face whose skin was as white as bone. He jerked his hands upward like a parody of surrender. For a moment any sense of reality dropped away.

I did not lower my aim. The man said something but his words were as senseless as those spoken underwater. We stood there for moments that I could not measure.

And then he gradually lowered his right hand to indicate that he had an inside pocket. I did nothing. His eyes were pleading for mercy and I thought that maybe his lips were, too. I hated him for his eagerness to surrender and his desperate need to live.

Slowly he eased the hand into the pocket. I thought that he could be reaching for a photograph of his girlfriend but I also knew that a prisoner might suddenly withdraw a hidden pistol and shoot his captor dead. I knew I couldn't take that chance. I knew I couldn't hesitate.

I fired. The round hit him hard and he fell over backwards so rapidly and so ridiculously that his feet could have been hinged.

I never told Debbie the full truth of what had happened.

I had once thought of telling Alex. Just before he left to go overseas I went for a drink with him and began to confess, but then I stopped. I would tell my son when he returned. But Alex would never return. A roadside bomb exploded beneath the wheels of his vehicle, tore it apart, and tossed its wreckage aside. Now I would never be able to confess to my son that I had once executed a captive. My Argentinian had been young, handsome, and unshaven, with frightened eyes. How could I have known that many years later he would return to invade my dreams?

'Whatever you say, the war was still worth it,' I tell Debbie. 'Maybe it's not your fault that you don't understand why. No one understands any more. People don't realise what's at stake.'

'You can think what you like. I can't stop you believing in things that aren't worth believing in.'

'And your new friend Vince agrees with you, does he? A man who's never had to fight a war – is that right?'

'Most of us have never had to fight a war, so that's a stupid thing to say, and you know that it is.' Debbie stands back to examine her work. 'You shouldn't try to annoy me. Never pick a fight with someone who could let you walk out with your hair part-done.'

A crazy part of me wonders if I should take the initiative and stand up and leave, no matter how the unfinished cut may look. But of course I don't. Instead we fall silent, and I pick anxiously at the slices of hair that have fallen on my sleeve.

After cutting for several more minutes Debbie announces satisfaction with her progress. 'That's better. Yes. All I need do now is tidy up the edges. And I'll sort out your ears, too. I'll use my little machine for that. And I'll do your eyebrows while I'm at it.'

She puts the scissors back on the table and plugs the clippers into a socket on the wall. The droning metallic buzz is close enough to sound threatening.

I use her name for the first time. 'Debbie.'

'What?'

'Have you invited Vince to move in?'

The clippers falter momentarily but then move on. Desperation silts my heart.

'He doesn't belong here,' I tell her.

'You can't hold back change.'

It's not the answer I want. It's not an answer at all. There's a taste in my mouth like a rotting tooth.

'Have you given him my key?'

'No. No, I haven't.'

The clippers crawl and buzz across my scalp as if I'm being prepared to join the ranks again.

'But you want him here, don't you?'

'I don't know. I really don't know. I'm not keen to invite anyone else to share my world. Especially after Alex.'

Vince never met Alex. I'm happy about that. I don't want him to have known our son.

'It's the past that makes us what we are,' I say.

'You're wrong. It's the present. What we shared is past. Our marriage is past. Even Alex is in the past now. And we've got to learn to live in the present.'

And I think of Vince, a man I have never met, swaggering into property that I still think of as mine.

Debbie takes the clippers from my skin and steps back. My head tingles slightly and my limbs are weak.

Strands of hair litter the sheet like plucked feathers from a bird.

'Eyebrows and ears,' she says.

She tilts my head as if it were inanimate and begins to slice away the tiny hairs on my ears. The cleaner's rotating blades deafen me. When she has finished Debbie lifts the scissors again and clicks them absent-mindedly as she studies my eyebrows.

'I always used to cut Alex's hair, too, do you remember? When he was in his early teens he was desperate to be fashionable. I had to keep up with all the latest styles.'

'Of course I remember.'

'I looked after both of you, didn't I? Helped pick your clothes. Told you what suited you and what didn't. Made sure you always looked good. And Alex *always* looked the best.'

'That's right, he did.'

Light trembles on the scissor blades.

'Don't move,' Debbie says as I involuntarily flinch, 'I'm not going to harm you.'

'I know,' I say; 'I know.'

But I feel exposed and vulnerable and think that even someone in an everyday situation, like having a haircut, could be easily injured or killed. I'm always having thoughts like this.

'There,' Debbie says after another minute or so, 'you look fine now.'

Her voice is suddenly thin. She clears her throat roughly before she goes on.

'You look like a soldier again.'

I am not sure that it is meant to be a compliment.

Debbie lifts the towel from my shoulders and gathers it together.

'I hope you're pleased,' she tries to add, but the words crack like ice beneath too heavy a weight.

I stand up and watch Debbie as she goes into the kitchen, bends to flip open the lid of a refuse bin, and shakes the gathering of cut hair into it. Afterwards she does not fully straighten, but remains slightly stooped and with her head bowed. I can hear the second hand of the kitchen clock as it ratchets across the numbers and divisions.

When Debbie speaks again her voice is thick, as if her throat is full.

'None of us can go back. We have to live with what we've got. The past is just the past. It's gone. We can do nothing about it.'

She raises her head and looks at me. Her face is set and her eyes have become suddenly angry.

'If I was offered a chance to go back than I'd take it,' she says. 'If someone came along and told me I could go back in time and change things then I would go. I wouldn't care about you or about me, I wouldn't care about anyone or anything else, I would only care about Alex. And I'd do everything I could to make sure that he was still alive. I'd sell my soul to do that, and I wouldn't care if it was to an angel or a demon.'

I don't know how to answer. Maybe I shouldn't try. A few stray hairs have fallen on my trousers and I brush them away as if it mattered.

'You don't understand, do you,' she goes on. 'You got used to a soldier's life; you got used to people being killed. It's *natural* to you – like part of the universe. But it'll never be natural to me. Alex needn't have been killed. His death was avoidable and unnecessary. He didn't save anyone or anything by dying.'

Debbie stops for a few seconds and it feels momentarily as if everything has been paused. And then she speaks again.

'Nothing will ever be worth the life of my son. You can tell me that soldiering is for any cause you can think of, but I'll not believe it. I'll always say that you got fooled. The two of you. You got *fooled*.'

But I think that she doesn't know much about either truth or death. Debbie's grief and her loss are a little imagined. She hasn't had to face death in the way that I've had to. I doubt if she's ever even seen anyone dead.

'You should go,' she says, as if everything between us has been exhausted.

I rub a hand across my scalp and feel the bristles. The cut has been close; just the way that I like it.

'I'll do that,' I say.

'I don't want you to come face to face with Vince.'

'Right.'

For a moment I stand there, for all the world as though I was expecting to be invited back home, and as if somehow life could be restored to what it once had been.

'Please leave,' Debbie says; 'leave now.'

She walks behind me to the door. Outside it is still raining. I put my coat and hat back on in a silence that seems to bulk around us. I don't know what to say, and instead I nod curtly. Even as I do that, I know it's wrong.

The moment that I step back into the drizzle the door closes behind me. Without thinking I check in my pocket for the keys, but I gave them up months ago. The damp air feels cold in my lungs and my scalp tingles a little.

I start walking. I think that maybe on the other side of the door Debbie has begun to cry again. It comes easy to her, but it's difficult for me.

After less than a minute a decelerating car drives past, its indicator flashing. Behind the sweep of the wiper blades a man's face can be seen through the smeared windscreen. He is middle-aged and undistinguished and I wonder if it is Vince. But I do not turn to see where the car stops. Instead I try to increase my stride and walk on. We'll meet face to face sometime. It can't be avoided. We'll sort things out then. Sometimes it's best to delay facing things.

I didn't fully understand what I was doing on that island, but I knew we were there because it was necessary. Besides, I'd signed up to fight whenever and wherever I was told to fight. I left the reasons to others. Maybe the dead Argentinian had been just like me. We fought and we died for an idea of moral right that we never really thought about and only partly understood.

He lay on the blank dark hillside with his head tilted back and his dead eyes staring up into dark low cloud. There was several days' growth of beard on his chin and for the first time I noticed that his unkempt hair needed cutting. As a colourless dawn edged across the sky his body seemed to gather its shape.

I bent down to study the hand that was slipped into his inside pocket. Only the wrist was fully visible. I pressed the clothing on his chest where a pistol could be hidden and it was wet with blood. There was no sign of any firearm.

I tugged at his arm and the hand slid free. A photograph

was clenched between his thumb and first two fingers. The blank side was facing upwards, and on it was written a message in a language that I did not understand. I took the photograph from the dead man's fingers and turned it over. It was a portrait of a man and woman in their fifties; his parents.

I put the photograph back in his tunic and pressed the sodden clothing back down on it. Light was strengthening and the man's face was taking on more detail and more personality. I turned away. I already knew too much about him.

He'd been terrified of death, I thought. My captive hadn't wanted to live and fight on that bleak cold island, miles away from home. He was there because he had to be. Maybe in those last few seconds he'd understood what things were really like. Maybe just before he died he could have seen in my eyes that I had cause enough to kill him. I believed that I was right and that I'd always been right. I had believed that justice was on my side. And maybe in those last few seconds my captive had seen that, too.

Nationalists

O N T H E D A Y that our daughter was ill I took my guns from the rack by the door and cleaned them. I make a habit of regularly checking and oiling the weapons; the routine calms me. Absorbed by the heft and texture of each component, and by the mineral small of oil, I am usually able to forget everything else. This time I could not.

During the night our daughter's fever had worsened, and my wife and I were forbidden sleep by her delirium. We tried to calm the girl but she was incoherent, as if the fever was burning up her mind as well as her body. I placed my hand on her brow. It was frighteningly hot and yet my palm came away marked by droplets that felt as cold as water from a spring. My wife raised her from the pillows while I tried to make them more comfortable to lie on. She whispered false confidences in our daughter's ear and then lowered her back onto the bed as gently as she could. Outside a convoy rumbled past. There are no street lights nearby; its way would be illuminated by moonlight and stars.

At dawn I woke a neighbour so that his boy could bring the doctor. The youth was churlish with sleep, and by the time he got on his bicycle I was already returning to my own house. The wheels squeaked as he pedalled away. The sun was just clearing a line of spruce along the far ridge and rabbits paused as light touched the fields.

My wife was bathing our daughter's face. It was pale with sickness and her hair was so damp that it formed little curls that had been pushed back from her forehead. A clock struck the hour.

'I've said he has to come straight away,' I said. 'If he does I'll be able to see him before I leave.'

My wife nodded distractedly as I cleared my throat.

'A country comes first,' I explained.

'Yes,' my wife answered absent-mindedly as she got down on her knees beside the bed. She pressed her hands together and closed her eyes. Her lips moved soundlessly. It took several minutes before she was finished and then she looked up.

'God will hear us better if you pray too,' she told me.

I got down on my knees beside her. Although I tried to concentrate on the crucifix on the far wall, my thoughts would not flow into the ease of prayer and I soon stopped trying. But I remained kneeling until my wife stood up.

'If I could sacrifice someone else to save her I would do it,' she said with sudden anger.

'Of course,' I agreed. 'We both would.'

'I think of all the things we denied her when we had no cause. A new dress for her birthday. A trip to the city. A necklace or a bracelet. She would have loved one of those. She likes bright things.'

'You're right,' I agreed, just to say something.

'Where's the doctor? He should be here by now.'

Panic made my wife's voice jagged, and she clasped our daughter's hand as if grip alone would prevent her from slipping into the next world.

I went outside to feed the animals, The chickens ran after the scattered grain, the pigs snorted and chomped when I filled their trough with slops, and the goats looked at me with eyes as impenetrable as glaze. For a while I envied their existence. I wished that I, too, was insensitive to everything but hunger. I loved my daughter, but a part of me hated her for being so ill, for making us suffer. Visions of her death and burial would not release their stranglehold on my imagination.

The doctor arrived in his car ten minutes later. As I met him at the gate I looked down the road to see if any trucks were approaching. None were.

The doctor was a fastidious, supercilious man with a beard that he had trimmed and shaped so that it curved gracefully just above the line of his jaw. I realised that he must have shaved that very morning. And I was filled with resentment that our child should have taken second place to his vanity.

'This is an emergency,' I said.

'I came as quickly as I could,' he replied, glancing at my militia uniform with a look of distaste.

'Our child could be dying.'

'I don't think so,' he said airily.

'She'd better not come to any harm, doctor.'

He stopped and looked calmly at me. For a second I was taken aback by his composure, and then he walked past me and into the house.

While he examined the girl I waited nervously, not

knowing what to say. Secretly I was terrified that some kind of revenge was being taken on my family, and that its youngest and weakest member was being allowed to die. The doctor worked in a silence that did nothing to reassure me. All the time my wife stood close, as if she feared that somehow he might cause our daughter harm.

Eventually the doctor stood up.

'There's nothing to worry about,' he announced.

In that moment I felt that I had taken my first breath for a long time.

'I've seen these symptoms in others over the last few weeks – high temperature, rapid pulse, a degree of inflammation, slight delirium, dehydration. The girl has an infection, a fever – unpleasant, worrying, but short-lived. It will pass within twenty-four hours. Treat her as you are doing, but make sure she doesn't become too warm. And be certain that she takes in liquid. See this?'

He pinched her skin between thumb and forefinger. My wife started forward and then stopped.

'It's as if it belonged to a much older person,' he explained. "Give her tiny amounts of tepid water, drop by drop if you have to. Try to make her drink too much and she'll just vomit.'

'There must be something else,' my wife said; 'some other form of treatment.'

'No. The main thing is to get her to drink a little and often. That will be enough. Dehydration is the only real danger now.'

I shook my head disbelievingly.

The doctor must have sensed my despair. His attitude

softened for a moment, and he spoke to me like a teacher gently patronising an unruly pupil.

'Your daughter will be fine. I'll return later if that makes you happier.'

'You despise us, don't you?' I asked.

My wife began to protest, but my anger was rising and I would not be diverted.

'You think we're barbarous fools, backward and super-stitious, incapable of compromise. Let me tell you, Doctor, that people like me are your protectors. You might under-stand the workings of a disease, but you don't understand what is necessary for a country's good health.'

He shook his head sadly. 'I have to go. I have other patients waiting.'

'And it doesn't matter to you what they've done, does it? They could be thieves, rapists, murderers.'

'I treat you all,' he said firmly. 'I've sworn an oath to do that. Most people round here don't seem to understand. That's a human tragedy. I've given up hoping that you will. That's mine.'

I walked back to his car with him. A truck painted in camouflage colours was driving down the road towards us. The doctor turned questioningly to me. I held his gaze.

'Surgery is sometimes necessary,' I explained. 'You of all people should understand that.'

He did not answer but got back behind the wheel and drove away. A hundred metres along the road his car and the truck passed each other as they headed in opposite directions.

I went back inside to collect my things and kiss my wife and daughter. A kettle was heating on the stove.

'Tepid,' I instructed, hoisting my rifle onto my shoulder.

My wife nodded but was annoyed. There had been no need to remind her of the doctor's advice.

I was the last of the militia to join the truck. Brotherly hands hoisted me over the tailgate. As clannish and eager as any hunting party, we sat shoulder to shoulder as the truck jolted along the unmetalled road. All our rifles were oiled, all our boots were polished. Someone told jokes and everyone brayed with laughter except me. I was still thinking of my daughter.

It seemed to take a long time to reach our target village. On its outskirts three old buses, scarcely roadworthy, stood in line with their engines idling and blue smoke puffing from the exhausts. Civilian drivers lounged against the doors with their sleeves rolled up because it was so warm. Our tailgate was unbolted with a crash. As we jumped to the ground I could smell burning. Scraps of blackened paper were lifting into the air like lazy buzzards.

A crowd of a hundred or so women and children sat in the open area at the centre of the village. They had been herded together like sheep. Every face was marked by shock and distress. Most had been weeping, but now they had fallen silent. They dared not move because our soldiers had them surrounded. Nearby a small bonfire blazed. White smoke boiled from it and ascended into the sky. I could see legal documents, books, photographs, and images of religious leaders curl and blacken in licks of yellow flame.

A little further away an old blanket had been stripped from someone's bed and spread out on the ground. Coins were scattered across it along with wallets, purses, rings, bracelets, watches, necklaces, lockets. The collection glinted richly, its gold and silver and precious stones catching the bright sunlight.

We stood beside our truck, rifles at the ready as if we had been present at the start of the operation and not its end. An army captain walked over to our leader, saluted, and gave him orders. While they talked I looked round, trying to take in every detail. I knew I was present at the renaissance of a nation.

The villagers must have given little resistance. An old man lay beside an open door, stretched out with his face upturned like a sunbather's, but his eyes were sightless. Further away another man lay as if he had just curled up in the dust and fallen asleep, but his hair was matted with blood and some had soaked into the dust beneath him, turning it a dusky rose. A woman was sobbing in a nearby house. As I watched, one of the soldiers came out of the doorway fastening his trousers. He wore a sheepish grin of achievement, and when others cheered him ironically he clicked his heels and bowed like an actor acknowledging his audience.

Along with one of the other militiamen I was given four large cans of petrol and ordered to take them up a hill to the far side of the village. We began to walk, a heavy can in each hand. They banged awkwardly against our legs as the fuel sloshed inside.

Near the last house my companion noticed a wooden wheelbarrow which had been turned on its side. We righted it, loaded the cans, and set off again. Dust shook from the planking as we took turns in pushing the barrow.

On the way we passed another group of captives, all

men, seated on the ground. An officer was questioning them and consulting a printed list of names which he held in one hand. The men's faces showed both defeat and an unreal, childish pride, but their wrists were lashed together with wire behind their backs. The wire was new. It shone clean and bright against the grubbiness of the captives' clothing and skin.

My partner grumbled all the way up the steep path, He complained that we were fit enough and patriotic enough to be given more important duties than this. All we did was clean up after the soldiery: our contributions would be overlooked when the histories came to be written.

For the sake of peace I agreed with him and instead we concentrated on pushing the barrow up the bumpy slope. It was cumbersome and poorly balanced, and near the top we rested for a few moments and looked back at the village. Our compatriots had begun to herd the women and children into the buses. Their thin, hysterical weeping drifted up to us. The bonfire of their possessions still burned. I grasped the barrow handles and pushed on.

Once past the crest of the rise we came to a broad clearing behind a line of spruce. Soldiers with wide, excited eyes were pacing backwards and forwards, unable to relax. Twelve captives were digging a wide hole in the ground. None of them looked up. They just went on digging, apparently without emotion. Everything was silent but for the noise of spades cutting into the stony earth. Already the hole was a metre deep.

An officer walked across to us. His face was flushed and he wheezed slightly when he spoke. We were ordered to unload the cans and leave quickly. Petrol slapped against the metal as we placed the cans on the uneven ground. As I stooped I tried to prolong the moment and memorise the faces and clothing of the men who were digging. The officer became angry; insisting that we had seen nothing here and had to leave straight away. We agreed and saluted, being careful not to even glance at the deepening hole in the ground. Within a few seconds we had set off back down the slope.

Eager to show off his knowledge or perhaps imagination, my companion told me that the captives would want to sing their anthem and that because we were a civilised race we would let them do it. I didn't believe him.

We neared the village. The buses had been driven away and the captive men on the ground were being forced to their feet. Because of their bound wrists many found it difficult to rise and they contorted themselves like madmen in straitjackets ordered to stand. Our soldiers kicked and clubbed them with rifle butts until they were on their feet. Now that it was empty, the wheelbarrow bounced on the track like a live animal.

It was late when I returned home. Long shadows dimmed the fields and the spruce trunks were as red as dying beacons. As I walked to the gate my heart tightened, and I paused at my own door like a stranger summoning the courage to enter.

My wife must have heard the truck, or she was staring at the doorway when I walked in. The seconds slowed until I felt they would stop.

And then, quite suddenly, I knew that the crisis had passed. The very air that I breathed was richer, cleaner.

'She's getting better,' I said. It was not a question.

My wife nodded. 'The fever had passed its peak by this afternoon,' she said. 'The doctor came back and examined her again. He kept telling me the worst was over. At first I didn't believe him, but when I could see that he was right I wanted to fall on my knees and kiss his feet.'

'Did you tell him where I was?'

'I said you were hunting. I don't think he believed me.'

'The doctor understands disease. That's all he understands.'

I walked to the door of our daughter's bedroom. It had been left slightly ajar so that my wife could keep watch on her. She lay in bed, exhausted but untroubled, her hair tousled about her face. I pushed the door open slowly so that it would not creak and then I walked into the room with the lightest of steps.

My daughter's breathing was calm, deep, and regular. I reached down and pushed a few strands of hair away from her mouth, taking care not to touch her skin. I did not want to wake her accidentally. My wife came to stand beside me. I put my hand into my pocket and we looked own in silence for a while. Perhaps, in turn, God was also looking down on us.

'I have a present for her when she wakes,' I murmured.

My wife looked up at me. Her yes shone like bright liquid in the gloom.

I shook my head. I would not tell her what the present was; my daughter would be the first to know when she woke up. But as I stood there beside the bed I found that I could not stop fingering the gold bracelet in my pocket.

Lexicon

WHAT SURVIVES OF past civilisations is far more than architecture and earthworks. Whatever we say and whatever we do have taproots that feed within deep layers of the past. In faraway lands tongues we would not recognise have already expressed our every thought. Other minds have imagined our dreams and traded them amongst peoples who saw no distinction between belief, history, and myth.

Let us consider an example. More than twenty-five centuries ago Anaximander of Miletus was convinced that humankind was not created in its present form but was instead descended from primitive, bestial ancestors, governed not by reason but by impulse.

My guest appears to be considering how to react when I mention this. She glances at the books on the shelves, perhaps checking that they are not all about the same subject, and at the poster and the original sketch on the wall. Perhaps she thinks they are keys to my character. It could be that she is worrying that she has misjudged me. In our previous meetings I have always been careful to present myself as informed but approachable. Maybe now she is wondering if my true nature could be academic, tendentious, and obsessively pedantic. But I will not be deflected.

'He also believed that our ancestors were themselves descended from fish – which is probably why he refused to eat fish. And the Greeks categorised their citizens according to the fish that they ate.'

'I thought you were cooking fish for our meal. Isn't that what I can smell?'

'You can indeed. Everything is going to plan. We'll begin with a feta salad first; just a small one.'

'Harry,' she asks with a kind of hesitant firmness, as though she needs to be certain that we are both in agreement, 'this is *just* a meal, isn't it?'

'Of course,' I answer, as if other possibilities had never entered my thoughts.

I should give my guest the honour of using her correct name. It's Heather.

'I've never heard of your Miletus person,' Heather admits. 'Should I have done?'

'Not at all. Should I go on?'

'If you want.'

'Of course I'll go on. I'm a natural pedant who never misses an opportunity to illuminate.

'He was one of a group of thinkers who lived on the coast of Asia Minor. The city was at a junction of trade routes so memories and folk tales and beliefs from across the known world will have taken root there. Nowadays we class them as a group, but Anaximander and Thales and Anaximenes all held differing opinions on, for instance, the prime constituent of life – one believing it to be water, another, air.'

It's obvious that the last thing that Heather expects from me is a lecture. And that is why I refuse to end it quickly. I like to begin my social evenings with some minor irritation.

'The one thing they had in common was that they were all dualists.'

'They fought duels?'

The hint of a smile tells me that she thinks no such thing. Heather is teasing me. I nod wryly to let her know that I have understood.

'I mean that they saw the world in terms of opposites – good and evil, truth and falsehood, appearance and reality, and, of course, civilisation and barbarism.'

'And I'm sure they all thought of themselves as very, very civilised.'

'Just like us,' I say; 'look at this house. Look at how I am able to live.'

I sweep my hand across my stylish and nicely appointed property. Heather is seeing it for the first time; I trust that she appreciates what she can see.

My home displays a certain degree of wealth, but it also displays taste. I might have inherited a small fortune but I worked hard to increase it so that I may live in such comfort and seclusion and without disturbance. I have developed my understanding of décor, of food and wine, of music, of books. I have earned enough to buy the original Michael Ayrton pen-and-ink sketch that hangs on the wall, and I have enough sense of harmony to balance it with the G F Watts poster from the Tate. Of course my life is full of secrets; whose life is not?

'I'm comfortable here,' I tell Heather. 'I hope that you are able to feel comfortable, too.'

'I didn't really expect you to live like this,' she says. 'Actually I'm not sure what I expected - not really. And I would never have found this house if you hadn't picked me up to bring me here. Those roads were like a maze.'

'I know them backwards,' I tell her, as if this did not matter. 'Well, I'm delighted that you're here at last.'

Of course she had not known what to expect. I have always been judicious in what I have told Heather. For several weeks I have known far more about her life than she has known about mine. She has talked a lot about her childhood, her work, her ambitions, and her hopes. Like all lonely people, Heather talks too much when given the opportunity. Sympathy and a little kindness are enough to encourage her reminiscences and confessions. All I ever have to do is express concern.

In many ways I am a tender creature.

Bound within his confine of masonry and rock, Asterius has made it a kingdom of the senses. He has touched, sniffed, and licked every part of the prison that is within his reach. For him the rough stonework and uneven floor hold countless variations of shape and texture. His hearing is pitched to the faintest of whispers – he can hear the quick rhythmic sighing of bats' wings as they swoop through the unlit chambers, and he is always aware of the distant oceanic pulse that insinuates itself along the outer passageways. And even at the very heart of his domain he can distend his nostrils and sniff the endless, brilliant, gull-bearing air.

And sight? Why, Asterius can see well enough. At the innermost chamber of the stone puzzle, where all light is dim and tentative, Asterius can still see. The pupil fills the entire eye.

'I think differently to you,' Heather says. The opinion is given with more force than the sentence requires.

I feign a lack of interest. 'Those are Kalamata olives,' I tell her.

'You shouldn't have gone to all this trouble. And I *do* know what a Kalamata olive is.'

'I *like* going to all this trouble. You're worth it, aren't you?'

She smiles demurely; she must have practised such a smile for years.

'And now you can explain why you believe that we think differently.'

Heather places an olive into her mouth, eats the flesh, expels the stone into her fingers, places it on a little saucer I had provided, and then continues.

'I think we met by chance – just chance. That's all. I imagine you don't believe that.'

'I see. And what do you imagine that I *do* believe?'

She toys with her glass. I begin to lift the wine bottle from its cooler and then I stop and let it slip back down.

'You shouldn't drink too much,' I tell her. 'Another glass with the fish, two at the most, and that should be enough. I've seen what drink can do so I'm always watchful.'

'I see. Do you always take such good care of your guests?'

'All of them.'

'You act like a relative – a guardian or an uncle.'

'It's true. That's what I am – a kind of relative.'

I sit back and study Heather for a few moments before I speak again. 'So then, why would I believe that we didn't just meet by chance?'

'Harry, I'll bet that you think it was fate. It's usually the other way round. It's women who believe in a kind of destiny and men think that things just happen by chance.'

'Do they?'

'Of course they do. But it's not that way with us, is it? There seems to be something unusual about us. I can't quite understand what it is but we don't seem to have . . . Well, I just expected things to go a bit differently. The balance between us isn't anything I've ever come across before. I like you, you like me, and yet we don't seem to have quite adjusted to each other, no matter how hard we try. Maybe it's because we actually see the world more differently than we admit. And maybe partly it's because you believe we were *destined* to meet. Is that right?'

I smile but say nothing. Heather goes on.

'But if you did believe in fate, then you wouldn't have to arrange things – because they would just happen anyway, wouldn't they? Everything would be determined and you couldn't alter that. You have all this Greek stuff going on in your head and *they* believed in fate. Or so I thought.'

I shrug. 'The fish is almost ready.'

'Well did they?'

I lean forward. Perhaps without thinking she leans further away as I explain.

'In the greater sense that everyone will die and that no one can escape death – yes, that's true. But also in the lesser sense in that the Greeks were convinced that everyone has a share, or part, or portion of life that is divinely allocated to them as their due.' After a pause, I add, 'Maybe you and I are due a part of each other's life.'

She shivers playfully. 'Don't say that. It sounds really creepy.'

'I'm just expressing what most people still believe. You probably believe it yourself without realising it. That kind of understanding is fixed into our imaginations and the way we look at the world. It's not modern - not at all, even if we think that it is. We're all just echoes of what others have thought and done centuries ago.'

'They fascinate you, don't they? The Greeks, I mean. Has it always been that way?'

'You want my life story?'

'Some of it, Harry - so far you haven't told me much.'

I look solemn as I speak.

'When I was a child I was ill for more than a year. It's all right; I got over it and there were no after-effects. But for a long time I was ill and on my own and felt deserted, so I read whatever I could find. I remember coming across a book of Greek myths. I know now that they had been censored and sanitised for young readers, because the originals are laced with murder and incest and rape. But for me as a child even bowdlerised versions were full of excitement and magic and mystery. I was fascinated. They were as real to me as the room I lived in, maybe more so. I have made my money in the modern world; my comfortable living is thanks to that. But it was the ancient world that took over my dreams, that sharpened my ambition, and that gave me a purpose.'

I pause. Most of what I have told her is true.

'You poor man,' she says; 'I had no idea.'

I shrug and look to one side because I do not want her sympathy. I want her fear.

'Is that why you have that drawing and that painting?' she asks.

'You recognise their subject?'

'I think so.'

'Ayrton catches the creature's power, I think, and Watts his poignancy. You'll notice the crushed bird beneath the hoof. Pausanias wrote that the creature's proper name was Asterius but no one calls him by that name. I often think about the citizens of the classical world. They lived in mythic times and they knew it. The oral tradition was paramount and they all knew their Homer. Some of them must have known that their own names would be passed down, generation after generation. And I wonder how it must feel to be in possession of the knowledge that your name will live forever.'

Heather shakes her head. 'I can't even think about things like that. *Our* names won't live, will they? We're not going to find them on lists of the famous – or the infamous.'

'Maybe not,' I say; 'but for me there's still time to make that list.'

And I put my hands together sharply to indicate that, for the moment, the subject is closed.

'Right,' I announce; 'let's get on to the main part of the evening. We'll be eating tuna, which was high on the list of approved foods. What they really liked were dogfish and eel, but I thought you'd prefer tuna.'

'You're right; I do. Thanks. I've never eaten the other two and I don't really want to.'

'No one in the Trojan War ever ate fish, of course. Roasted meat was the meal fit for heroes. But we're not heroes, are we, Heather? We're somewhere further down the scale, midway between gods and beasts.'

'That's all right with me. I don't want to be heroic.'

Asterius on the rock platform that overlooks the sea. Today he has trapped a gull when it settled on the ledge. He has no need of the creature, but merely crunches its beak and bones between his jaws, and spits it out uneaten. Companion birds rise squealing from the cliff and from battlements high above come human cries of terror and disgust. The shape of his body, its hunched knotted shoulders and weight, make Asterius unable to turn and glare upward, but he is glad to have the loathing and cowardice of fools. He knows they believe him to be untouchable, his shape and his habitation not only a curse but visible evidence that there are worldly forces so extreme that they must be sanctioned by the gods. His most secret fear is they will forget the divine, and begin to think of him as absurd.

Only one passageway leads to the platform. Asterius uses it to keep his home clean, to dispose of bones, and to gaze out across the dazzling layers of sea and sky until his eyes ache. He has developed timetables for these actions, a calendar of routines, as he has developed times of the day or night that he can use for study and contemplation. He has read the works of natural philosophers, of poets, of travellers and soldiers; they are provided to him as he wishes, and the manuscript scrolls are lodged carefully on a rock shelf free from the mice that sometimes enter the cave and that he traps and eats. Asterius knows he is a cultivated man who can never be judged as such: instead the world will condemn him forever as brutish and ugly, a beast with scant traces of the mother who bore him, a half-animal barbarian dwelling among blackness, carcasses and ordure.

His kingdom, too, has a reputation for madness and incoherence, and yet the reality is that it is geometrical, logical and complex. Asterius has paced every step, not hundreds of times but thousands. He has bellowed out in echoes its distances and heights. Where others stumble in a bewilderment of possibilities, Asterius recognises clarity and symmetry. His home is no chaos, but an expression of harmonious and subtle order – the same order, perhaps, that makes the sun reach into his labyrinth, track across its outer walls, and then withdraw; the same order that brings predictable changes in daylight and weather across the year; the same motion that governs the great wheel of stars that rotates in the night sky. Throughout the night hours he often sits within his platform watching the stars, and sometimes tears run down his matted cheeks because of the cool, untouchable beauty that he believes only he can comprehend.

Throughout the meal I study Heather with expert intensity. I listen to the slight rustle of her clothes as she leans forward, the tiny click of an earring pendant as she tilts her head, the flat muted clack of her heels on the wooden floor as she adjusts her posture. Without her knowing it, I assess the texture of the skin on her hands and forearms, her neck and face. I recognise that her hair is thick but that it parts easily and is likely to be slighter coarser to the touch than many would expect, and I know that she has washed it earlier this evening. I am able to identify the shampoo that she chose as I can also name the perfume she has dabbed on her wrists and neck, but I can smell something beyond those markers; I can smell her skin. And when I distend my nostrils and half-close my eyes, I am sure that I can smell the processes of her body.

She places her fork on the plate and the noise grates. 'That entire meal was delicious,' she says. 'I had no idea you would be such a good cook.'

I nod graciously. 'I should confess that it's a favourite of mine, too. I've cooked it before.'

'For other people you invited here? Other women?'

'A few. A man, too. You have your predecessors.'

'Harry, you're being deliberately mysterious. I don't care who you've invited here. It has nothing to do with me. After all, we're just friends, aren't we?'

'For the moment,' I tell her, and I notice the very slight change in her expression as her imagination begins to work.

To prevent my following up that remark, she takes a sip of wine and holds the glass in her hand as if it were a kind of shield. And then she decides that this is not enough, that she must give a strong signal that she is preparing to leave.

'It's getting quite late. I'll have to say goodnight soon.'

'Of course. Will you have a coffee before you leave?'

'It keeps me awake.'

'It's already prepared. And don't worry about the time; I'll take you where you have to go.'

She hesitates. I bring the tiny cups across to the table, and as I am walking back I see that the position of her legs has altered and that she is ready to stand up at any moment.

'Here,' I say, 'this is the genuine article.'

She tastes the coffee and cannot stop herself from making a face. 'It's terribly strong.'

'There are grounds in the bottom that will look like silt. Most call it Turkish, but there's no love lost between those two countries.'

She becomes sisterly. 'Harry,' she says, 'I understand why you got into all things Greek, but don't you think you're taking it a little too far?'

I shake my head. 'It defines me. It's central.'

Heather pushes the cup away. 'I'm sorry but it's far too strong for me. And I really should be going. I don't want to inconvenience you. Maybe I should ring for a taxi.'

'There's no signal here; you'd have to use my landline. Don't worry, I have everything sorted.'

Again she tenses. I stretch out my arms as though taking an exercise, and then relax them.

'You were right,' I tell her, 'I do believe in fate – of a kind. You may think that we met by chance, but I know that we didn't.'

Her eyes become fixed on me. I can see the tautness in her shoulder muscles.

'I picked you out,' I confess. 'I chose you, I followed you, I tracked you. By the time we met you knew nothing at all about me, but I already knew a great deal about you.'

'Harry, you're making me nervous.'

'Really?'

'Tell me this is some kind of joke.'

'No, I'm serious. And by the way my name isn't Harry. Oh, that's the one I used for you, but I've already been a Tom and a Dick. If I use a well-known sequence it makes matters so much easier. I could be John next time, and then

Paul and then George. I don't think Ringo is workable though, do you?'

She stands up and the chair legs squeal across the floor. Her face has turned pale.

'You lied to me,' she says.

'How quick on the uptake you are,' I murmur.

'I'm going,' she says firmly. 'I don't know what you're playing at but it's beginning to frighten me.'

I put my hand on my heart and heave a theatrical sigh.

'Harry, or whoever you are, whatever was between us is over now. Tell me where your phone is and I'll ring for a taxi. Once I'm out of this door you'll never see me again.'

I smile neutrally. I am already prepared to move very quickly.

'The door is unlocked and the phone is in the next room,' I tell her; 'but maybe you realise by now that I gave you a fictional address for this house.'

Trembling and with a pallid face Heather takes one step backwards in readiness to turn and run. She does not understand that I have already assessed her body's mass and resilience and that I know how easily she can be brought to the floor. And I have something else to say before she moves.

'I'm afraid, my dear Heather, that you have no idea where you are or what is about to happen to you.'

She races for the door. Immediately I am out of my seat and after her. A plate with its cutlery crashes to the ground. My sense of timing is perfect. She reaches out for the door handle but never touches it. No one ever does.

◊

Asterius and the offerings. In earlier years he hated his imprisonment so much that he delighted in playing with his victims. At lengthy intervals the massive iron-studded door that separates the labyrinth from the palace would be opened by men with spears, and instead of his usual food a group of terrified youths would be thrust into the dark. The door would be slammed shut and on its other side huge bolts would be pushed home. The sacrifices were left alone in an unfathomable blackness, cold and with the reek of a farmyard, but beyond that, perhaps a promise of the distant sea. In those days Asterius stalked his prizes, snorting and roaring to increase their terror, refusing to trap them as easily as he could have done.

He has killed so many that he is no longer consumed by rage. His hatred of humankind has abated, and everything seems melancholy to him now. Asterius has changed. He has grown older. For a while he believes himself to be a sensitive ogre, a creature much misunderstood, a beast given at first to gentleness and consideration before he is overtaken by rage and driven to do what is necessary.

He drives his victims near to the rock platform, and only when they can see the daylight and are racing towards it does he bear them to the ground; sometimes they are even within a few strides of that long but survivable leap into the sea. Their disgust and terror infuriates Asterius, and he couples with them in a brutal parody of his own conception. He does this with both the women and the men; as long as he can find an opening in the body he does not care. Usually his weight cracks their ribs, but if not he breaks one or two of his victims' limbs and watches while they crawl towards the daylight that they still mistake for rescue. The air streams against their faces, they can hear the calls from the fishing boats, and most bitterly of all they can see and hear the soaring, indifferent birds. By the time they reach the outer edge of the platform Asterius is always there to drag them back, to disable them further, to couple again until he is exhausted. Only when he is sated and bored and guilty does he allow them their deaths. It is at moments such as this that Asterius realises that he has already become a legend.

My smile is hesitant, maybe even a little shy. The young woman looks directly at me and gives a quiet smile in return. She has yet to be convinced about me. Her caution will not be a difficulty. I always work slowly to achieve my ends.

'I'd better tell you my name,' I say; 'it's John.'

Asterius and the life beyond. Because he is steeped in learning and myth, Asterius is aware that his own destiny is also to be murdered. His due, his divine allowance was to be given only a certain amount of time, and its end will coincide with his betrayal.

The butcher enters his domain, sidling through the dark corridors as he follows a guiding thread. As his death draws near, Asterius feels jaded and weary of the life he has been fated to lead. The entrance of his killer into the labyrinth is no surprise; in a way, he welcomes it as a culmination. For Asterius is aware that his fame will live on. He may be known less by his true name than by a description, an appellation, but this will be spoken ten thousand times more than the name of his mother. And as for the identities of his many victims, they will have been long forgotten. Asterius will become part of a vocabulary of myth, forever recreated, forever invoked. He will have entered a list of the great, a lexicon of those so famous that their names can never be erased.

At the moment of his slaughter, as his head is lifted to the blade, he understands that his only immortality is this form of remembrance.

But for all his ambition and for all his dreams, Asterius has a mind that is more specific, more isolated and more restricted than he is capable of recognising. Perhaps this is why he imagines that both in the barbarism of his life and the savagery of his death he has achieved an apotheosis. As the light fades in his eyes he finds consolation in that thought.

Of his victims, Asterius thinks nothing at all.

Daniel's Skyline

L IKE ANY OTHER proud mother I have kept all of my
son's work from the day when he first went to school.
At the bottom of the wardrobe in his bedroom there is a
cardboard box filled with wallet files, and tucked into each
folder are drawings, mementoes, school reports, and short
pieces of writing. Photographs of him, like some of his old
clothes, are kept separately.

He is the only person I have done this for. Only a few
traces remain of my husband - a handful of wedding and
holiday snapshots, our marriage certificate, our decree
absolute. An archivist would discover only fragments of
my married life, because most of the evidence has been
deliberately destroyed. With Daniel it is different. For him,
an entire biography could be constructed from what has
been collected and retained. Thinking that it might do
some good with his assessors, I have even let them borrow
his work as evidence.

Before visiting Daniel this afternoon I looked again at
the folders. I found it distressing. I sat with the contents
fanned out around me, achingly aware that each clumsy
image, each badly-written word was from a time beyond

recovery. The future, whatever it is, can only be darker, and its horizon ever closer.

Just before puberty Daniel wrote an essay. It took him a long time to write. He visited the library by himself and noted down details which he transcribed exactly. I did not discourage him; neither did his teachers. We were all pleased to see him take such an interest. And besides, at the time, it did not seem that a boyish fascination would become an lifelong obsession. The essay reads like this –

New York is the greatest city in the world and the tallest. It is made of skyscrapers. The skyscrapers reach so high they scrape the sky. Everybody looks like ants. They run around. The skyscrapers are 100s and 100s and 100s of feet high. When I grow up I will live in New York. I will have a house on the top of the tallest skyscraper. I will never go back to the ground. There is the Chrysler building. There is the One World Trade Center. There is the Empire State that King Kong climbed. There is the United Nations building it is glass and steel. There is the Seagram building it is smoky glass and aluminium. When I am on the top of my skyscraper I will see over the whole wide wide world and never never go back to the ground where I was born.

He signed it with his name, house number, street, and the name of an English city. I still live at the same address.

My son never became sensitive about his childish work. He had no need; it differs only slightly from work he produced later. Much of this is written in notebooks which are still kept on a shelf in his bedroom. He has not slept in that room for some time, but I have changed nothing. Like the guardian of a shrine, all I do is maintain it.

His walls are covered with posters of New York. The images are of the most recognisable kind – the Statue of Liberty, the Brooklyn Bridge, Central Park and, most of all, skyscrapers. The risen skyline flattens itself against Daniel's walls. In the high summer shots the buildings are hard-edged, with windows etched deep by the angle of illumination; in autumn a thin bronze veneer coats the verticals and reflective surfaces glare in the sunset. Perhaps most magically of all, at two in the morning the city is massed blackness and geometric constellations, as if a god had scissored the night sky, folded it into uprights, and stacked it shoulder to shoulder around streets ribboned with headlights.

Daniel's books are undisturbed, too. Most of these are picture guides to the city. And there are several DVDs, some of which he has watched over and over. I have sat with him while he compulsively viewed favourite sequences again and again, as if they held secrets which only repeated study would make clear.

On the inside of the door he has fixed the postcards sent by his father – no more than four a year, always with a hackneyed tourist image of the USA on the picture side and an uncomplicated greeting on the other.

For a while Daniel's father lived in New York; later, he sent postcards from other parts of the country. He never gave his address.

He left before his son was two years old and before

Daniel's condition was confirmed. I was pleased to see him go; I don't want to meet him ever again. I just wish he would stop sending the cards. Once or twice I intercepted them and tore them up, but conscience made me hand over the later ones.

I sometimes wonder if the early postcards, simplistically garish as they were, were the keystones for our son's fantasy and craving. I don't think Daniel wants to meet his father; he has no interest in the man. It is the city that occupies his imagination.

Daniel has never been to New York. I don't expect he will ever go, and neither will I.

The assessment centre lies on the far side of a town fifty miles away from our home. Beyond its high perimeter fence there must have been small fields, but the hedge-rows were grubbed up long ago and now there is only a featureless range of grain.

A few weeks ago, when Daniel was first sent here, I stood in an interview room on the upper storey and gazed through the smoked glass. I pretended to be absorbed by a distant farmhouse and a solitary line of trees, but in truth I saw little. I hoped that the angry trembling in my limbs was not visible, although for several minutes I could not control it. When I had composed myself and turned back, I realised that the only impression I had retained of the view was of an immensity of sky.

I had already complained that Daniel was being assessed too far away from where he lived. No one actually dismissed my fears, but the doctors were urbane, aloof, uncaring. Distance from home was hardly a relevant factor,

I was told. And besides, one possible result of the investigation was that my son would be placed in a detention centre even farther away. After all, the investigation had found him guilty.

The apparent reasonableness of that statement, and its emphasis on the word *guilty,* as if no other verdict had been possible, made something lurch inside me.

This morning it was different. Daniel and I were alone in our booth, separated from the staff by clear screens. A camera fixed in a high corner watched us all the time.

We sat at either side of a table that resembled an interrogation bench. The table top smelled of antiseptic spray. I thought of the dozens, perhaps hundreds of other mothers and sons who must have talked across the same barrier.

I reached out and tried to clasp Daniel's hand, but he moved it away from me. I asked him how he was. He did not answer. Instead he ignored the question and stared to one side, apparently taking in nothing.

He was far too young to be in such a place, I thought. No matter what his chronological age, he was far too young.

'You have to take care of yourself,' I said. 'Living here must be very hard for you.'

Daniel jerked his head, caught my gaze for a fraction of a second, and then looked away again. 'Home,' he said.

'But it's not home, Daniel. Not our home. And it's not the other one that you used to live at. You were among friends there. This place is completely different. There are people here who are studying you. It's their job to decide what happens.'

Suddenly he became preoccupied with his fingers, and

began to interlace them as if he had just discovered a new trick. I watched him for a while. Big though Daniel was, I wanted to pick him up, take him home, comb his hair and brush his teeth and make sure he was dressed properly. No one was doing that for him now. True, he had attempted all of these things, but ineffectively. His hair was parted in two uneven swatches separated by a ragged line, his breath was stale, and he had been dressed in clothing that was too big. The collar of his shirt was so wide that it made his neck appear thin and his head too large. He looked so out of place, so vulnerable, that I had to concentrate hard to make sure that tears would not come to my eyes. He hated to see me cry.

'Can't you get someone to help you?' I asked.

'What?'

'You know, with combing your hair and things like that.'

'I'm a man. A grown man. There's, uh, no need. Not for that.'

I nodded. 'Right. So. So what's happened to you over the past few days, Daniel? Have they been testing you every few days?'

'Yes, that's right. Every day. Uh, think.'

He still could not look at me. I was used to this. Daniel never held a gaze. He was incapable of it.

'Listen,' he said suddenly, and cocked his head. As he listened to a noise I could not hear, small tremors ran through him and made his head sway.

'I can't hear anything,' I confessed.

He raised a hand and extended one finger as if in admonition, but I wondered if he was pointing upwards.

I strained my ears to listen. In common with others who share his condition, Daniel has excellent hearing. All that I could detect were a few indistinguishable muffled noises from elsewhere in the building.

'Boeing,' he said with a smirk. 'New York flight.'

Of course there was no way he could know where the plane was going, but I thought it probable that he could hear the engine noise, and possible that he could identify it. I was very still and tried not to breathe for a few seconds. Then I believed that I could sense a distant murmur, far, far away but it may have been a wish to hear, nothing more.

'It may not be going to New York. It may not even be going to America,' I said.

Daniel nodded vigorously and struck the edge of the table several times with his fingers. 'Heathrow to JFK on the regular schedule, distance 3475 miles from central London to, uh, *Daily News* building.'

'Right,' I agreed. Any resistance to such determination was merely token.

'The plane I take.'

'One day.'

'Soon. I'll take it soon.'

'There are a few things that have to be sorted out here first, Daniel.'

There was a pause. I knew he would ignore me.

'That's why they're keeping you here,' I went on. 'The people who are interviewing you, the people doing all those tests, all those measurements, they're doctors.'

'Yes. Right.'

'Clinical psychologists: men and women who are trying to find out what kind of person you are. Whether or not you're dangerous. Whether or not you can be trusted to live in the outside world.'

Petulantly, Daniel arched away in a part-spasm.

'I'm doing my best to help,' I insisted. 'I've told them what a good son you always were; how I've always been proud of you, how you'd never hurt anyone. I've always insisted on that – that you'd never hurt anyone. But my word isn't enough. They won't believe me. They want to do their own tests, reach their own conclusions. What they decide—'

'Take that plane soon,' Daniel interrupted, his hand drumming irregularly on the side of the desk, 'sooner than, uh, than anyone thinks.'

I soothed him. 'Maybe you'll do that one day when this is all over.'

His eyes rolled upwards as he tilted his head toward the ceiling. I knew he was listening for another plane, or any kind of distraction, but that he could hear nothing.

'They believe her, you know,' I said cautiously.

Apart from a quivering of one arm, Daniel did not move.

'I don't think you meant to do anything. I'm sure you were just experimenting.'

A look of concentration invaded his face, as if he were willing a plane into existence.

'I know you didn't mean to hurt the girl,' I continued. 'I don't think you did hurt her. She panicked, that's all.'

'No more,' he said sharply. It was a demand that we stop discussing something he found unpleasant and unsettling. Throughout his life he had been liable to fly into a rage if forced to confront a consequence of his own problems.

'You have to talk about this, Daniel.'

He said nothing.

'You have to tell the doctors that you'd never been with a girl before. You have to tell them that you didn't know what was going on.'

Still no reaction.

'You have to convince them that you just wanted to see what she really looked like, that was all. It was something new for you, wasn't it?'

I do not know if he shook his head or nodded.

'They have to be convinced that you were just a couple of curious adolescents. If things had been different it would all have passed off quite normally, just like it does like for most people, just like it did for me and your father.'

And for the first time in months I thought of a few defining minutes with the man I had married - the ridiculous, unsettling festival lights that played on the side of our hotel; the reeling shouts of holidaymakers in the streets outside; the humiliating, intertwining rhythm of breath and bedsprings that I was sure would permeate the building; and, at the moment when I longed most sharply for escape, the sound of a single-engine aircraft flying tourists on a half-hour trip along the holiday coast. When he had finished he lay on top of me and gave a little snigger of self-congratulation. I stared at the ceiling, listening to the engine fade, and knew that everything had changed.

Daniel had been conceived on that very night. For several months, I thought he would be my rescuer.

'No more,' Daniel repeated, this time in an agitated manner. His hand twisted and leaped on the table like a landed fish.

'If you can't talk to me about it,' I asked, 'who *can* you talk to?'

He turned in his seat. I thought he was about to stand up and leave. I spoke his name quickly, and reached out to touch his hand. He pulled it away.

'You must be very careful what you say,' I told him. 'You must convince everyone that you didn't mean any harm.'

'Didn't harm her. I didn't.'

'I know it, Daniel.'

'Was just—'And he stopped and moved his upper body again.

'Curious,' I repeated.

'Curious,' he echoed. 'Yes. That's right– I was just, uh, curious.'

I had imagined the scene many times. A large Edwardian conservatory had been attached to the home in which Daniel had lived until a few months ago. Beneath a high glass roof rows of tropical plants were growing; some had been there for so long that they were as large as small trees. Daniel used to take me to see them. Everyone loved the plants, the teachers had assured me; their shapes, variety, colours and scents made a visit to the conservatory both stimulating and therapeutic. But the humidity had taken my breath, and the jungle of greenery was so thick that there was a feeling of menace about the place.

It was in the conservatory that Daniel had supposedly assaulted the girl.

Even now it was impossible to find out what had really happened. Not much, I suspected – some fumbling, yes, and perhaps a little sexual exposure and maybe touching, but nothing violent, nothing threatening, nothing invasive. The girl hadn't become distressed until afterwards, and by then Daniel himself was upset and tearful.

'What made you stop?' I asked, although I already knew the answer. Like his intellect and his character, Daniel's sexuality would never fully develop. To him it would always be a puzzle, a mild pleasure, perhaps even a threat, but never a fulfilment.

'Didn't stop,' he said.

I waited.

'Didn't stop,' he insisted. 'I wanted to, uh, to go on. That's what should happen. You should go on.'

'But she stopped you?'

'She, uh, didn't like me. Scary, she said. She said I was scary. Me. She said I frightened her.'

Daniel looked at me for a moment. For a second he was an ordinary young man, rejected, hurt, possibly vengeful. He was just like the rest of us.

And then I saw in his eyes, quite clearly, that he was beginning to make his escape from me, and that nothing I said would bring him back.

'I'll not take *her*,' he said decisively, turning away again.

I shook my head. 'No. She won't want anything to do with you.'

'I'll go on my own to New York.'

'Yes. That would be a better idea.'

'One World Trade Center also called Freedom Tower, 104 floors, 1776 feet high. Chrysler Building, 1046 feet, twelfth tallest in the city.'

'That's right.'

'Empire State, 102 floors, 1250 feet, 1454 feet with

antenna. So high you can see mile after mile after mile. As tall as that.'

'Right again, Daniel.'

'All in New York, every one of them. A city made of skyscrapers. I'm going to live there soon. You know that —. yes, you know that. Hundreds, hundred, hundreds of feet high. On the very top you can watch the sun go down and people in the streets tiny as ants running around. I'll be happy there.'

'Yes Daniel,' I agreed; 'on the very top.'

I am sitting on the floor in Daniel's room. A letter lies beside me on the carpet. Outside it is dusk.

When I arrived home the letter was behind the front door. Although I have not opened it, I recognise the hand-writing. It is from the man I once married. It is postmarked New York and it is addressed to Daniel. I want to tear it up unread but instead I drop it on the floor.

I am sitting in a kind of museum to Daniel. All around me are his displays— dramatic, changeless, and chosen. I press the play button on the TV and the screen fills with images that are black-and-white, high contrast, silvery. I watch for a few seconds and then look around the room.

Everything here is a guess at reality, a chance, a dream. It is not a recreation, not a representation, but a work of fiction. Whatever the letter says I know that it, too, will be an invention.

Often I wonder if our entire lives are governed, not by what is real, but by what we are able to imagine.

I have seen the film many times - the expedition's arrival at the island, the huge gates, the chosen sacrifice, the gigantic monster touching his blonde prize with tenderness so clumsy that it will be mistaken for an attack.

I take one of Daniel's notebooks down from its shelf. Laboriously, exhaustively, he has copied down fact after fact about his city - materials, dates, addresses, tonnages, dimensions. I leaf through the notebook, ignoring the letter at my feet.

Tormented beyond endurance, driven by something he can never be capable of explaining, the monster ape scales the vertical walls. An excited crowd gathers in the street below and gasps in horror when be plucks the girl from her room.

As he heads ever higher, the girl clasped tenderly in his fist, single-engine aircraft fly towards him across the risen skyline. Moment by moment, building by building, they close in on him as he reaches the summit.

Afterlives

I T WAS A year of disasters. There were floods in Italy, forest fires in the South of France, and an Icelandic volcano blasted ash so high into the air that it drifted towards Europe. But for me it was also the year in which a better, happier life opened up, and with Kate I was content.

Of course I still had to deal with Zoe. Her phone calls were often unexpected, usually made when I was with Kate, and either wheedling or aggressive. Despite them I still hoped that she would agree to a rational division of our possessions, property and savings.

And then one afternoon she phoned when Kate was at work. I held the phone away from my ear as I paced out the measure of my new home. Zoe's voice was so insistent it was easy to believe that she stood beside me in the room.

That day she was conciliatory, a little nostalgic, and eager to remind me of good times we had shared. And in a comment that made me instantly suspicions, she wondered if I had found that living with another woman was just as I had imagined. And then she added that Kate wasn't really *right* for me – but of course she understood why I'd been attracted to her: Men were like that; they strayed. And then she added that some women were forgiving enough to welcome back their lost sheep.

I didn't comment. After a few silent seconds Zoe reminded me that she still kept her car parked on the road outside. Wouldn't it be a good idea if she drove to see me to talk things over? In fact she could set off now – yes *now*, this very instant.

I insisted that she not do that. Kate would be back soon and would hate it if she found Zoe sitting at her home. And besides I thought it would be the wrong thing for Zoe to do, because she and I would probably just fight.

And I knew she would say *But Michael* and begin to list reasons, all spurious. I told her again it was a mad idea and that I wasn't going to discuss it any further. And I pleaded with Zoe that it would be foolish to get into the car. In fact, I said, before things went any further it was best that I end the conversation now.

She started to say something else but I told her firmly not to ring back and I ended the call before she could respond.

I switched on the answerphone and waited for her to ring back, but all was silent. After a short while I played some music to relax and began to prepare food for Kate's return.

Half an hour later Zoe drove her car at high speed into the back of a lorry. She was killed instantly. It could not be decided if she had been driving recklessly, had had a seizure of some kind, or even if the crash had been deliberate.

I went to the funeral and sat at the back of the

crematorium because I knew that all of her relatives and most of her friends would think that somehow Zoe's death had been my fault. Unwilling to meet them, and not sure of what I would say if I did, I crept away unnoticed. As my old lover was being cremated I was already on the road back to her replacement.

Of course I was happy with Kate. It was not that I had forgotten Zoe; I had no intention of doing that. But death placed a frontier around her memory, fixing it so that it was no longer capable of development. Subject to contract our house had been sold, and once that transaction had been finalised I would completely free of her influence.

Of course there were photographs. Kate considered it essential that they be kept because otherwise I would be denying my own history. And at unexpected moments my recall became suddenly vivid, such as when I picked up one of the expensive glasses I'd brought with me and found the faintest trace of Zoe's touch on its curvature.

I was on my own when Kate's landline rang. When I had walked away from Zoe I had also walked away from my job, so I hoped that the call could be an offer of employment. I'd had some exploratory enquiries but nothing definite, and more than once I'd been confronted by silence, as if a call had failed or someone had changed their mind. Thus time I picked up the phone without checking the incoming number. A woman spoke. Her voice was too intimate and too unreal.

'Is she there?'

My strength drained away within seconds.

'I said; is she there?'

'No,' I answered, although I was not convinced that I had actually spoken out loud.

'Good. We can talk.'

I was so weak that I could not reach a chair, so I lowered myself to the floor.

'This can't be you,' I said. 'You're not alive.'

'If I'm not alive, Michael, how can I be talking to you now?'

'I went to the crematorium. I saw your coffin.'

'And you crept away like a burglar, didn't you? You couldn't face either my family or my friends.'

'You saw me?'

'Of course I saw you. And I've been watching you ever since. You follow that woman around like a faithful dog. It's embarrassing to see you treated like that.'

'Where are you, Zoe?'

'Where do you think I am? I'm where you left me – at home.'

'Our house?'

'That's right,' she said firmly, 'at our home. Have your already forgotten where that is? You'll have no difficulty finding it again because there's an estate agent's sign in the garden. It won't take you long to drive here.'

'You want me to come back?'

'I'll expect you home soon.'

The line went dead. I checked the number but it had been withheld. And then I struggled to my knees and phoned the number of the house that Zoe and I shared. Just as I had requested, the line had been disconnected.

I rang Kate at her work and told her I had to go out. She was puzzled and asked why.

'The agent called about the house sale,' I lied. 'Some sort of problem with the contracts. I'm going to see him now, I won't be long.'

'Michael, it's an eighty-mile round trip. There's no good reason for you to drive all the way there and all the way back. A phone call could sort it.'

'It will put my mind at rest. Don't worry. I'll be as fast as I can.'

But I drove towards my old home like a man driving into the unknown.

A *Sold* placard stood undisturbed in the garden and the house was in darkness. I unlocked the front door and pushed it open. A chill touched my throat. Beside the telephone there was a small pile of circulars that someone must have picked from behind the front door.

'Zoe?' I asked.

There was no reply.

'Zoe?' I said again, more firmly this time. Nothing greeted me but silence.

Of course there was a rational explanation for the circulars having been moved. The new owners wanted to take measurements for changes they planned to make and I had authorised the agent to give them access. They must have picked the mail from the doormat.

A fine scattering of dust coated the surface of the telephone. I scored a track through it by running a finger along the edge of the cradle. Then I lifted the phone and held it to my ear. It was completely dead.

I switched on every light in the house and went from room to room. Twice I called out Zoe's name and each time it faded into the silence. There was no trace of her at all, but like a superstitious fool I checked the back garden, cupboards, and behind closed curtains, I wanted to be utterly certain that I had overlooked nothing. Finally I returned to every room, switched off each light, and closed and locked the front door behind me. When I got back in the car I discovered that I had become short of breath and could not immediately start the car.

Kate was waiting for me when I returned. 'Is everything all right?' she asked.

Yes,' I said. 'It's all fine.'

'And the contracts?'

I walked away so that she could not see my face. 'It was just a typographical error. You were right; I needn't have gone all that way.'

She asked no further question but I could sense that she doubted if I had told the truth.

Later I decided that my exchange with Zoe must have been a hallucination, a kind of mental dislocation, but that there was little to worry about. My imagination had created a fictional narrative around a phone call that I had probably not even answered. That seemed to be a satisfactory explanation: I had read accounts of sane, well-balanced people holding imaginary conversations when they were ill or stressed. That could have been me It was even possible that I had picked up an infection or virus that had temporarily disrupted my perceptions.

The next day Zoe phoned again.

'You didn't come. I was waiting.'

'That's not true. I came but the house was empty.'

'Do you expect me to believe that? I'm sitting here now, still waiting. You didn't even ring back.'

'The landline is disconnected. I checked.'

'Really, Michael, if you're going to lie then at least have the decency to tell a believable lie. How could I be speaking to you now if this phone didn't work? And what have I done to deserve such treatment? I was good to you, and yet you repay me by running off with that woman. She'll be tired of you soon; surely you must know that. Now that you've had your fun you should come back to me. It's where you belong.'

'New owners are moving into our house, Zoe. I don't know where you are, but you're certainly not there.'

'Do you think I can't read an estate agent's sign? But you can't have me evicted because the sale isn't legal. I haven't signed away my half of this house.'

Knowing that Kate would be back soon I looked at the time. Tension raised my voice.

'You don't exist, Zoe. You drove into the back of a lorry and were killed instantly. Sometimes I think that you did it deliberately.'

'You'd be a fool to believe that I would kill myself because of you.'

'But kill yourself you did. You're not alive anymore. You're just a container of ashes poured into the ground of a memorial garden.'

'How do you expect me to react when you say things like that? You're sick, Michael. I'm flesh and blood. I'm the woman you lived with and ate with and slept with. I'm not a figment of your imagination.'

'But that's exactly what you are. I don't know why this is happening. I must be ill in some way that I don't understand.'

'If you're going mad it's because you've only just realised how you've wrecked everything. Leave that woman,
Michael. Come back to me and forget her. I'm not going
to let you go. Where is she now?'

'Working, but she'll be back within the next few
minutes.'

'And you'll still be looking for work because you were
stupid enough to leave your job just like you left me. She'll
be happy with that because she's made you dependent on
her. Really, everything is so obvious.'

I heard the front door open. Without saying more I
pushed the button to end the call. Kate came into the room
as I replaced the phone on its cradle.

Immediately it began to ring again.

I stood motionless. The noise drove like a squall through
the house. Kate looked at me curiously.

'You're the nearest,' she said, as though she detected
my guilt.

I had no choice. Gingerly I picked up the phone.

Zoe was frighteningly quiet. 'You can't get rid of me
as easily as that. I'll make you face up to your responsibilities. And, Michael, you *will* tell her that I called, won't
you?'

I ended the call.

'Who was that?' Kate asked.

I could not tell her the truth because she would never
believe me. She would think me insane. I felt dizzy and ill.

'A woman keeps ringing me up,' I said. 'I don't know
who she is. She doesn't leave a number.'

'I see,' Kate answered dryly. 'Why don't you leave it
on answerphone permanently? Or, better still; give your

mobile details to this mysterious woman? That way you'd be certain that I wouldn't overhear your intimate conversations.'

I knew that to reply would only make things worse.

She said no more about it, but from that moment on I knew that as each day passed Kate became more and more suspicious.

For a short while all was quiet, but I was always expecting an attack and never strayed far from the landline. And then, inevitably, it rang when Kate was with me. We stood facing each other as the noise drilled the air.

'You look guilty,' she said.

The answerphone was triggered but no one left a message and the line went dead.

'Number withheld?' she asked.

'Yes.'

'Michael, your secret life is affecting us both. Don't you want to tell me the truth?'

'It's just a woman playing games. I don't know why, I can't be responsible for what she says.'

'There's no point in continuing with that lie. I can see straight through it.'

'I'm not lying.'

'It's humiliating to be treated like this. It can't go on. I have to think it through.'

The phone rang.

Kate's face registered her anger. She turned away, ready to walk out of the room. I snatched up the phone, almost dropped it, but took hold of her upper arm with my free hand.

'It's Zoe,' I told her, grasping her tightly so that she could not break free.

'Let me go.'

'That's the truth,' I said. The release of confession coursed through me. 'It's Zoe who has been ringing me – *Zoe*.'

'You're crazy,' Kate said. She tried to squirm away but I held her even more tightly.

I lifted the phone to my ear. 'Zoe?'

And Zoe answered.

'Michael, why are you still there? We both know you should be here with me.' Still grasping Kate by the arm, I held the phone to her ear. 'Speak to her,' I demanded.

Her eyes were frightened and uncertain, as if she now saw me as someone who had become unrecognisable.

'It's the only way you'll believe me,' I insisted. 'Once you've heard her speak I'll let you go.'

For a few seconds I believed that Kate would say nothing, but at last she spoke into the receiver.

'Who are you?'

I could hear no reply. Kate spoke again.

'What's your name?'

Her face was full of contempt as she thrust the phone back to me. Quite suddenly she twisted her other arm to break free. Knowing that I was hurting her, I let go.

'Your friend is too scared to answer,' she said.

I tried to prevent her from getting away by placing a hand on her shoulder, but she immediately stepped farther back.

'Zoe?' I said unto the phone, but the line was dead.

'Michael,' Kate said, 'if your new friend needs you to

visit her than maybe you should do that. But don't come back here.'

'I don't have a new friend and I don't want one. It's Zoe. She must still be at my old house. She's waiting for me.'

Kate shook her head.

'Come with me,' I said.

'No. You're ill, Michael.'

'I have to go. It's the only way she's going to stop tormenting me. Come with me.'

But Kate stood looking at me as if I had become a stranger.

The route from Kate's house was constricting and irrational because of a sudden unnatural gloom. It seemed like a much later hour, and when I checked the time I was surprised to find that it was still early evening. I had to use headlights to cut into the darkness, and on the main road cars drove towards me through a grainy fog.

At my old home the agent's sign had been laid flat on the grass as though abandoned, but what I noticed most keenly were the lights that burned in the downstairs rooms. My hand shook at the front door and it took me three or four attempts before I could fit my key. There was no need. The door was already unlocked.

The hallway lights were on. I could hear a murmuring, conspiratorial noise, like something being discussed in secret. I paused for a moment and then, like a man wounded, I called her name.

'Zoe!'

The murmur stopped.

I called again, less certain this time, but her name hung

in the room like an afterglow. Suddenly there were rapid footsteps. My heart constricted.

A man appeared in the doorway to the living room. A woman followed him. The man was holding a mobile phone as though about to call and the woman had something metallic in one hand. I had never seen either of them before in my life.

We stared at each other, dumbfounded.

'Yes?' the man said at last.

'What are you doing here?' I asked.

'What do you mean?'

The woman spoke. 'We own it,' she said; 'it's our house.'

I continued to stare at them. 'We *own* it,' she repeated.

They were both wearing old jeans and shorts, and I now recognised that the woman was holding a retractable steel ruler.

'You bought it from me,' I said stupidly, and saw them relax. 'How long have you been here?'

'Just today,' the man said. 'We're measuring up. It's our second visit. The agent said that would be all right so we borrowed a key.'

'Don't worry,' the woman added: 'we'll be signing the contract in a couple of days.'

'I'm not worried.'

We continued staring for several seconds until I spoke again.

'Have you had the phone reconnected?'

The man answered. 'No, but if we decide to still have a landline—'

'It would be useful,' the woman said. 'If we do, we'll get a different number,'

I nodded but my head was aching.

'Do you want anything?' the man asked.

'Yes,' I said. 'When you arrived, was there a woman here?'

They glanced suspiciously at each other and I wondered if they were a little frightened.

'No,' the man answered.

'Just us,' the woman added.

'Listen,' I said, 'if a woman should call—'

But then I stopped.

'I'm sorry,' I continued, 'I shouldn't have bothered you.'

I turned and walked out into the darkness feeling feverish and weak. The man tried to tell me something else but I scarcely heard him.

There were no stars and the night seemed to be a weight pressing on the earth. I got in the car, closed the door, and saw that small unidentifiable particles were clinging to the windscreen. As I steadied my hands on the driving wheel I turned on the wipers and washers. Greyness smeared the glass before it was swept clean. The car started at the third attempt and I drove away.

After a while I began to realise that the tyres were not gripping the surface as they should and that the engine was beginning to labour. I dipped the headlights and saw that the road was scabbed with shallow patches of greyish material scored by tracks.

I almost missed the turn to Kate's house. Even when I had taken it I suddenly began to doubt if I was on the correct road. Every perspective was distorted and flecks like grey snow fell ever more thickly on the windscreen.

Soon I was lost. The car juddered to a halt near a turn in the road that I could not remember. There was no signpost and I had no idea where I was. Everything around was muffled and quiet.

I got out of the car and stood beside it. Greyness sifted through the air and breathing became difficult. I looked around for an identifiable landmark but could see nothing. Feathery particles fell without cease through the choking darkness. I did not know which way to go. I did not know what to do.

When I walked in front of the car I stirred up grey clouds that hung suspended, like sand disturbed beneath the sea. Ash fell all around me, covering the car, the road, the fields and, somewhere unseen, Kate's house.

I looked upwards and saw nothing but blackness. Out of it the ash fell gently, determinedly, endlessly. When I licked my lips I could taste it on my tongue.

Acknowledgements

THESE STORIES HAVE previously appeared in *Best British Short Stories* 2011 and 2022, *Critical Quarterly, Granta Shorts, Interzone, Leviathan, The Minerva Book of Short Stories, Prospect, Resurgence, Telling Stories, Les Temps Modernes, The Time Out Book of New York Stories, Underwater, The Warwick Review,* in chapbooks by Clarion Tales and Nightjar Press, and on BBC Radio 4.

This book has been typeset by
SALT PUBLISHING LIMITED
using Granjon, a font designed by George W. Jones
for the British branch of the Linotype company in the
United Kingdom. It is manufactured using Holmen
Bulky News 52gsm, a Forest Stewardship Council™
certified paper from the Hallsta Paper Mill in Sweden.
It was printed and bound by Clays Limited in Bungay,
Suffolk, Great Britain.

CROMER
GREAT BRITAIN
MMXXIV